Cast of Ch

Jeff Troy. A self-styled detective w
long. Right now he's working in a photographic studio.

Haila Troy. An actress who's currently between jobs.

Anne Carstairs. An old friend of Haila's. But she doesn't seem very glad to see the Troys move into her Greenwich Village apartment house.

Scott Carstairs. Her husband, a struggling commercial artist. He's keeping a lot of things from his wife.

Polly Franklin. Another tenant at 39 Gay Street. She owns a thriving restaurant a few blocks away.

Ward Franklin. Polly's brother.

Mike Kaufman. Another tenant. His body is found in the Troys' garden after being drowned in their bathtub.

Henry Lingle. A retired art dealer, also a tenant.

Charlotte Griffin. Another tenant, a stout, middle-aged lady who's very protective of her bedridden sister Lucy.

Maude Revere. A very attractive children's book author. She and Scott have a secret.

Jacob Bruhl. A former detective.

Mr. Turner. The landlord, a rabbity little man.

Lieutenant Hankins. A homicide detective. He suspects Jeff had something to do with Kaufman's murder.

Bolling. His assistant.

Charley. The janitor.

Books by Kelley Roos

Featuring Jeff & Haila Troy

Made Up To Kill (1940)
If the Shroud Fits (1941)
The Frightened Stiff (1942)
Sailor, Take Warning! (1944)
There Was a Crooked Man (1945)
Ghost of a Chance (1947)
Murder in Any Language (1948)
Triple Threat (1949)
One False Move (1966)

Other mystery novels

The Blonde Died Laughing (1956)
Requeim for a Blonde (1958)
Scent of Mystery (1959)
Grave Danger (1965)
Necessary Evil (1965)
A Few Days in Madrid (1965
(Above published as by Audrey and William Roos)
Cry in the Night (1966)
Who Saw Maggie Brown? (1967)
To Save His Life (1968)
Suddenly One Night (1970)
What Did Hattie See? (1970)
Bad Trip (1971)
Murder on Martha's Vineyard (1981)

The Frightened Stiff

A Jeff & Haila Troy Mystery by
Kelley Roos

Introduction by
Tom & Enid Schantz

Rue Morgue Press
Lyons / Boulder

The Rue Morgue Press
P.O. Box 4119
Boulder, Colorado 80306
800-699-6214
www.ruemorguepress.com

Printed by
Johnson Printing

PRINTED IN THE UNITED STATES OF AMERICA

The editors wish to acknowledge the invaluable contributions made by Stephen Roos
to the writing of the introduction to this edition.

About Kelley Roos

AGATHA CHRISTIE gave us the first husband and wife detective team in her second book, *The Secret Adversary*, in 1922, but the idea of using a married sleuthing team on a regular basis didn't really catch the fancy of other writers—and the reading public—until Nick and Nora Charles made their memorable appearance in 1934 in Dashiell Hammett's last novel, *The Thin Man*. Hammett did not write any other Nick and Nora mysteries, although he worked on some of the six screenplays featuring the hard-drinking, sophisticated sleuths that played in movie theaters from the late 1930s into the early 1940s.

The couple's popularity on film no doubt helped inspire Patrick Quentin to create his New York theatrical sleuths, Peter and Iris Duluth, who debuted in 1936's *A Puzzle for Fools* and were featured in a half-dozen other cases into the 1950s. Next up were Jake and Helene Justus, those rye-soaked Chicago amateurs who aided and abetted lawyer John J. Malone in a series of very funny novels by Craig Rice, starting with 1939's *Eight Faces at Three*. One year later, Richard Lockridge and his collaborator wife Frances turned a pair of Manhattan sophisticates he had originally created for a series of non-mystery short stories published in *The New Yorker* into martini-guzzling, cat-loving sleuths in *The Norths Meet Murder*. Like Nick and Nora, Pam and Jerry North were better known to most of the public because of their appearances in other media, notably in a couple of long-running radio and television series. Their 26-book run as married sleuths was equaled by Pat and Jean Abbott, the creations of another *New Yorker* writer, Frances Crane.

5

Pat and Jean met in 1941's *The Turquoise Shop* but did not marry until the end of the third book in the series, *The Yellow Violet*, in 1942.

Mostly forgotten today was another husband-and-wife team, Jeff and Haila Troy, who made their first appearance in *Made Up To Kill* in 1940, the same year the first Mr. and Mrs. North mystery hit the bookstores. Like the North series, the Troys were the collaborative work of a husband-and-wife writing team, William and Audrey Roos, who combined his last name with her maiden name to create their literary persona of Kelley Roos.

Why the Rooses and their series are largely forgotten today is a mystery itself, because at their best, as in *The Frightened Stiff* or *Sailor, Take Warning!*, they were the equal of—and perhaps a good deal better than—their more famous contemporaries. The Troys were funnier than the Norths, livelier than the Abbotts, often more involved in doing the actual detection than the Justuses, and a more convincing couple than the Duluths. Much of the couple's cheerful charm is on display in *A Night to Remember*, a 1943 slapstick comedy based on *The Frightened Stiff*, in which Loretta Young plays Haila (inexplicably renamed Nancy) and Brian Aherne portrays Jeff, who has been transformed from a jack-of-all-trades to a mystery writer.

The first eight books in the series, published during a nine-year span between 1940 and 1949, are light breezy affairs typical of the period in which Jeff does most of the detecting—or most of the meddling, as New York homicide cop Lt. George Hankins might put it—while his actress wife Haila narrates the action and occasionally spots the pivotal clue or rushes in where only fools and amateur sleuths dare go. A ninth book, *One False Move*, appeared seventeen years later, in 1966, with the couple unaged but now divorced (they reconcile). In tone, it somewhat resembles their other post-Troy books, in which suspense and psychological issues replace detection, though much of the good old humor is still present. Although *The Blonde Died Dancing* in 1956 did not feature the Troys, it was an expanded version of a Troy novelet in which the names of the couple were changed. It too was filmed, in France, in 1959, as *Do You Want To Dance With Me?* with Brigitte Bardot portraying the renamed Haila Troy.

Another non-Troy book, *To Save His Life* (1968), was turned into a highly regarded made-for-TV movie entitled *Dead Men Tell No Tales* in 1971. The Kelley Roos team wrote the television script for *The Case of the Burning Court* in 1960, based on the novel by John Dickson Carr, for which they won an Edgar from the Mystery Writers of America. Their other connection to filmed drama involved writing the novelization of *The Scent of Murder*, the 1959 movie in which the ill-advised technique of Smellovision debuted and died.

While their post-Troy books were often well-crafted crime novels, occasionally probing the mind of the killer and showing that the Rooses were changing with the times, the Jeff and Haila Troy series remains their legacy.

"The Troys were a lot like my parents," explains their son Stephen Roos, an accomplished author himself of a score of light, humorous books for kids. "They laughed a lot, drank a lot too. They worked very hard at their writing, but they never looked on their work as art. It was fun. They were entertainers. They loved great acting and great writing and they loved meeting actors and writers and making friends with them. They could be killingly social but they could spend a year at a time in Europe happily restricted to each other's company. They worried too much about money; sometimes they were next to broke but only sometimes. But not once did either one of them ever consider getting a real job. It would have ruined everything. They grew up in an age when the couple was celebrated in fiction as well as in real life and I think that's what they were about mostly."

William Roos was born in Pittsburgh, Pennsylvania, in 1911. His parents died when he was around ten and he was brought up by his German-born grandparents along with his older brother and younger sister. He first attended Allegheny College in Meadville, Pennsylvania, before transferring to Carnegie Tech in Pittsburgh to study drama. He started out as an actor but later became more interested in writing and began writing light, comic plays.

Audrey Kelley was born in Elizabeth, New Jersey, in 1912, but moved with her family to Uniontown, Pennsylvania, in her teens. She attended Sullins College in Bristol, Virginia, but, like her husband, transferred to Carnegie Tech to study acting.

It was there that Rooses met and fell in love. Although Audrey was still interested in pursuing a career in acting, William had decided his future lay in playwriting. However, he lacked one of the most important basic skills needed for his profession. He couldn't touch type. His solution was to pay Audrey's way through touch-typing school. After she successfully completed that course of study, they were married in November 1936 and, like other would-be actresses and playwrights, moved to New York City.

Unlike Haila Troy, Audrey's acting career didn't go anywhere. Following the birth of her daughter Carol in 1938, she decided to try writing as a career, focusing on mysteries because she had heard that it was possible to make a living writing them. Besides, she was already a great mystery reader, inspired perhaps by the work of a fellow Allentown resident, John Dickson Carr.

How the collaboration was born between Audrey and her husband isn't known, although their son suspects it came about while they were relaxing over drinks at the end of the day. Audrey would describe her mystery plot and William would make suggestions. Finally, one morning he started rewriting her first chapter and the collaboration was born. Their first book, *Made Up To Kill*, was published in 1940 by Dodd, Mead to favorable reviews and went on to a paperback edition. They received a $500 advance from Dodd, Mead.

In the early years of their collaboration, they would spent two or three months plotting the book and an equal amount of time on the actual writing. One would work on the even-numbered chapters, the other the odd-numbered chapters, then they would turn their chapters over to the other for rewrites.

However, as the years passed, raising their two children—Stephen and Carol—took up more and more of Audrey's time. While they continued to plot the books together, William now did the entire first draft himself, turning it over to Audrey for the final edit. He still couldn't touch type, so Audrey always managed to get the last word in. On one memorable occasion, Audrey discovered that William had decided on his own that someone other than their designated murderer would be the actual killer in *Requiem for a Blonde*, explaining that he had fallen in love with the original killer and couldn't bear the idea of her going to the chair. Audrey pointed out that this turned all of their carefully planted clues into nothing more than red herrings. In the end, as usual, she prevailed, although she was persuaded to commute the killer's sentence to life in prison.

If Audrey was busy raising the kids, William did all the housework He not only naturally was compulsively neat, but he'd do just about anything to actually put off writing. Besides, as Audrey explained, she was too busy doing all that touch-typing to bother with making the beds or washing the dishes.

When he wasn't working on their mysteries, William continued to write plays. His first play closed after five performances. His second, *January Thaw*, ran for only six weeks in New York but became a high school staple. He wrote the book for the 1948 Mike Todd musical, *As the Girls Go*, which had a year-long run in New York. He and Audrey collaborated on a mystery play, *Speaking of Murder*, which ran for a month in New York but did better in London.

After a dozen years in New York City, the Rooses sold their brownstone on East 93rd Street and moved to a late eighteenth century farmhouse in Connecticut. Carol left home for college in 1956 and Audrey, William and Stephen moved back to New York City for a year. Eventually they moved to the south of Spain where they mostly lived for the next ten years.

In the late 1960s, they bought a whaling captain's house on Martha's Vineyard, the locale of their last mystery novel, *Murder on Martha's Vineyard*, where they lived until their deaths. Audrey died in 1982 and William in 1987.

You won't find their names among the giants of the genre but their contribution to what that other Allentown mystery writer—John Dickson Carr—called the "Grandest Game," deserves not to be overlooked. They showed, as son Stephen put it, what it was like to be young and in love in the New York of the 1940s and, perhaps even more importantly, that mysteries were meant to be fun.

Tom & Enid Schantz
Lyons, Colorado
January 2005

CHAPTER ONE

I STOOD STARING about the room, and the first disadvantage of living in a basement apartment occurred to me. Jumping from a window would bring no release.

Cobwebs, heavy and thick enough to grace a Class A haunted house, hung from everywhere a cobweb could possibly hang. Half-burned papers and trash littered the hearth of the fireplace. And huge dust mice chased each other ferociously around what was to be the Troy bedroom. The apartment had been vacant several years, but even then the dirt must have kept its nose smack against the grindstone to get itself piled so high.

Charley, the little janitor, shuffled uneasily under my baleful glare and looked wistfully toward the door and freedom. "I didn't expect you to move in until next week, Mrs. Troy," he said.

"You don't remember," I asked, trying to keep the tears out of my voice, "our conversation last Thursday? I said may we move in October first. You said yes. You said you would have everything spick and span. Your very words, Charley, don't you remember?"

"Now I do," Charley admitted.

"Didn't you tell Mr. Turner?" Mr. Turner was our landlord. A nice man. He wouldn't let this happen to a new tenant who had paid a month's rent in advance. He lived in the building, but he had been away last Thursday. So I had talked to Charley; I had overestimated Charley. "You must see Mr. Turner every day," I said. "Didn't you tell him Mr. and Mrs. Troy had changed their plans?"

"My wife's been sick," Charley explained.

"All right," I said, giving up. "I hope your wife is feeling better. Is Mr. Turner home now?"

"No, ma'am. He's at one of his other houses."

"Charley, I bet if you have this place all cleaned up before he gets back, Mr. Turner won't be mad at you for forgetting."

"It's almost suppertime. I'll do it first thing in the morning."

Before I could point out to Charley that Jeff and I were going to start living here tonight, a Western Union boy stepped into the open doorway. "Super?" he asked.

Charley left me for him gratefully. "Huh?"

"Telegram for Mrs. Jeffrey Troy," the boy said. "But there isn't any name like that in the vestibule."

"I'm Mrs. Troy," I said. "We're just moving in."

I tipped the boy and ripped open the wire, expecting it to be from some pixie friend wishing us the best on our opening night at 39 Gay Street, New York, New York. But I was wrong, so wrong. *Axle broke at Westport*, the telegram informed me. *Will be delayed four five hours. Grayvan Lines.*

Charley had escaped while I was reading the bad news. I was alone, so I orally and enthusiastically damned all axles, moving companies, cobwebs, dust mice, Charleys, and finally myself. For it was all my fault.

If I hadn't accepted an engagement to act at a summer theater, Jeff and I wouldn't have sublet our apartment in town and taken the house in Connecticut. We would be moving from our old apartment on Ninety-Third Street to Gay Street. No axle would have broken in Westport, our furniture would be here. When Jeff came home from work at Photo Arts, I would have had everything shipshape, cocktails in the shaker, perhaps even something resembling dinner on the stove. But now—

"Is this where I live?"

"Jeff!"

"The boss sent me home early to help my wife get settled. But—" He looked around questioningly. I handed him the wire. Then I told him about Charley's forgetfulness. He put his arms around me and kissed me. "Poor Haila," he said.

"And poor you," I said. "This is your apartment, too."

"Well, we're both better off than that axle. Haila, listen! Walking over here from the Fifth Avenue bus I had the strangest feeling that I was doing something I had done a thousand times before. Why, I even turned into this place automatically. Without looking at the number."

"You've never been here," I said pointedly.

The point being that I had had to apartment-shop without the slightest help from Jeff. Shelter, food, and clothing were items that Jeff always took care of tomorrow. The only reason he had a respectable job at the moment was because he had never worked in a photographic studio before and he didn't want it to be said that he had never worked in a photographic studio. Or it might have been the models. I often wished I could be sure. Because in my day I had been a model—while looking for a job on the stage. And I could be a model again in a pinch.

Jeff was shaking his head in wonder. "It's as if I were coming home again. After twenty years. Well, Haila, show me around. I'd like to know all the exits and entrances. In case the joint is raided."

"This joint won't be raided," I said bitterly. "It'll be cited for soil conservation. You are now standing in what will be our bedroom."

He looked around the big room and his eyes turned doubtful as they lit on the two front windows. Their sills were on a level with the sidewalk, although a good three feet back, and only some rusty iron bars separated us from the pedestrians.

"I'll be happy sleeping here," he said. "But tuck me in carefully, or I'll wake up some morning with my head on the pavement."

"It won't be the first time such a thing has come to pass. This way, please."

He followed me into what, as far as I could see, was our new apartment's only irremediable drawback; the middle room. It was large and square and windowless. A little light filtered in from the open bedroom door and a little more from the living-room arch, but not enough. You couldn't thread a needle by it. But I could do without threading needles, and Jeff couldn't thread one under a Klieg light.

"Hmm," Jeff said, peering and squinting more than was necessary, "what is that over there? Something?"

"A door! A big white door. Leading to the bath."

"We'll have to serve each guest with a Seeing Eye dog."

"Jeff, when you get an apartment with a garden, there's bound to be some inconvenience!"

"Haila, I like this place, it's wonderful!"

"You're the one who insisted on a garden. You wanted to feel the rich loam slipping through your gnarled fingers."

"I admit it, darling. Readily. I'm a loam lover. As my father before me. He used to carry it around in his pockets." Jeff opened the bathroom door. He stood there, looking puzzled. "I've got that feeling again. I've been here before. Often."

"Bathrooms are curiously alike. The world over."

"I mean the whole apartment—this address. Thirty-Nine Gay Street. I guess I must be wrong. Let's see the living room."

"You won't like it."

He pulled me to him and put his arms around me. "Sweetheart, I know it's a hell of a job to move and I appreciate what you've done. We're going to have more fun living here than we would at the Plaza. We can run barefoot here. Now, as I love you, shall we split a kiss?"

"Needless to say."

"Then we'll look at the living room and take a stroll in the garden."

The living room, up two shallow steps from the rest of the place, was low-ceilinged and cozy, with oyster-white walls and a parqueted floor. The far side was almost a solid sheet of glass, casement windows and French doors that opened onto the garden. A great stone fireplace filled another wall, leaving just enough room for dark oak bookshelves to squeeze in on either side. The kitchen, small but adequate, was off to the right.

"Nice," Jeff said. "Nice fireplace. Does it work?"

"Of course. We can toast marshmallows."

"Did you pack those marshmallows?"

"There were only two or three left, but I did."

"No wonder that axle broke."

Jeff swung open the French doors and we went out into the garden. It was the width of the brownstone house and about thirty feet long. Back yard was more the word for it. Except for the lanky sumac tree that leaned against the fence for support, and a fountain, there were no attempts toward the beautiful. But that fountain was a thing! In a concrete bowl stood a concrete boy clutching a concrete fish to his manly little breast. From the mouth of the fish protruded a pipe, from whence, no doubt, water had once bubbled merrily.

I began to dream out loud. "Tulips, dahlias, sweet peas, jonquils, marigolds—"

"Uh-uh," Jeff said. "Carrots, onions, beans, corn, pumpkins, a couple acres of potatoes—" He crouched down and scooped up a handful of sandy dirt and pebbles. "First thing in the morning, I'll order a load of manure."

"Manure!"

"Don't be embarrassed, darling."

"And how are you going to get it in here?" I demanded.

He looked at the ten-foot fence that encircled the entire yard. It was unbroken by any gate or door. He turned slowly in the direction of the apartment.

"Oh, no, you don't, Jeff! Nobody's going to bring a load of manure through *my* bedroom!"

"I'll have them deliver it during the day."

"Absolutely no!"

"There isn't any other way to get it in. It'll have to come through the bedroom."

"It'll be delivered by parachute or not at all."

"Oh, all right," he conceded.

We were recrossing the middle room when Jeff abruptly slowed his six feet one inch of what he claimed was living steel to a halt. He gazed in annoyed bewilderment at the defunct fireplace that had been turned into a china closet.

"Haila, I know I've been here before. I've lived here!"

"Lived here? Darling, lack of food has probably affected your mind. Let's go and eat. We've got hours to kill. It may be midnight before those movers get here."

We had just stepped into the hall when I saw the girl on the stairs. Her head was bent and the curly chestnut-colored hair tumbled over her face, completely hiding it from view. But I knew that quick walk, the set of her shoulders, the way her arms swung at her sides the moment I saw her.

"Anne!" I shouted.

Her head came up with a jerk of surprise. Then a smile started in her large, dark eyes and spread slowly over the perfect oval of her face. "Haila!"

When we had finally untangled ourselves from each other, I introduced Anne to Jeff, admitting that he was my husband.

"Stop bragging." Anne laughed. "You aren't the only girl with a husband."

"Not you, surely! I never thought you'd hold still long enough to get married. Who is he, Anne? Do I know him?"

"Scott Carstairs is the name, and you don't know him, Haila. But you will, I hope. Everybody should know Scott."

I still was overcome with the suddenness and unexpectedness of our meeting. "Anne, it's been so many years! Where have you been? And what are you doing *here?*"

"I live here."

"You live here?" I squeaked. "Here?"

She looked puzzled. "Why, yes. On the third floor. We've been here for a year now."

I couldn't withhold my whoop of delight. "Anne! Jeff and I are just moving into the garden apartment. We're neighbors again, Anne!"

Not until I had waited three or four seconds for her exclamation of pleasure did I realize that none was coming. There was no gladness at all in Anne's face, only a lightning-quick flash of dismay and then that, too, was gone.

"Why—why, how perfect!" She smiled again, but it was a different smile, a forced and stilted one. "We'll have wonderful times, won't we? Just like the old days!"

"Yes," I said. I was too bewildered by the reception of my tidings to do any better. But Jeff rushed in and saved what was rapidly shaping up as an awkward pause.

"Anne," he said. "Haila and I are just going to dinner. Why don't you come along? You and Scott?"

"I'd love to," she said glibly, "but I really can't. I have an appointment uptown. And Scott has a class tonight. He's an artist and he's studying at the Art Students League. I hope you haven't married an ambitious man, Haila. Darling, you're looking swell! In a play?" Anne didn't wait for me to answer, she rushed on. Her voice was mechanical and stilted now, like her smile. "If you're eating here in the Village, you must go to Polly's. Of course you've heard about Polly's, on Grove

Street, just across Seventh Avenue. Polly lives in this house, too. Franklin's her name. A wonderful person!" Anne glanced at her watch. "I've got to step on it, I'm late! You'll forgive me, won't you? See you tomorrow, won't I?"

And she was gone. As I watched her flying up Gay Street, I felt the blood rush to my ego. I was confused and hurt.

All the way to the restaurant I kept trying to figure it out. Anne, my old pal, had been frozen by the idea that we were to be neighbors. But that couldn't be. She was the girl with whom I had played house and hookey, trotted off to boarding-school, traded clothes and beaus and secrets; she was the girl next door. Anne and I had grown up sharing even the same dream. We were going to be actresses when we got big.

Coming to New York we had split a little apartment on Fifty-Ninth Street and side by side we had gone timorously around the town, knocking futilely on managers' doors. Then it began to happen that I was pounding the pavements alone. Anne was having herself some fun. So much fun that her name made the columns. She was being seen in the wrong places by the right people, saying good evening to the milkman and good morning to the night watchman, cocktails for breakfast and the hottest new hotspot on toast for dinner. About all I saw of Anne were her orchids in the icebox.

Then I got a small part in a road show, a season of it. That separated us, of course, and somehow in the years that followed we lost each other, as completely as only old friends can. But I could find no reason for Anne's strange hostility at our reunion.

Jeff pulled me out of my trance. "Here we are, Haila. Let's go in and see a fellow tenant."

Polly's, a onetime carriage house, was spacious and crowded and noisy. A big cannel-coal fire blazed picturesquely, if needlessly, in a huge stone fireplace and its reflections bounced brightly off the bottles and glasses behind the man-sized bar.

Miss Franklin was obviously out to please one and all. One wall of the room was banked with high-backed booths for reticent or indiscreet couples. Then there were tables, open and aboveboard, for the unashamed, the frank and exhibitionistic. In the center was a large round table for the family trade or the dinner party.

Locating the proprietress herself was no problem; she was everywhere. Plopping a trayful of Martinis on a table, making room for newcomers where there was no room, rushing in and out of the kitchen's swinging doors, stopping here and there to recommend a dish or greet a friend. And everybody seemed to be her friend.

Polly Franklin was a wonderful thing to see. She was anywhere from thirty to forty-five. A genuine blonde, not dyed-in-the-wool. Her hair was that bright-gold shade never quite achieved by dissatisfied brunettes, beautifully unkempt, windblown by wind and not by educated fingers. Her face had a scrubbed and shiny look—Polly needed no makeup, and her laugh rang out contagiously above the din.

We were on our cigarettes and coffee when a ringing phone brought me back to my own life and its problems. "Jeff, I'm going to call the company now and order a telephone."

"We don't want a phone. They ring."

"I'll get one that whistles."

It wasn't until I had dialed the business office that I realized it was after hours, but I waited a moment just in case. And then, suddenly, I became aware of a voice in the next booth, a man's voice, thick and heavy. A few of the words he spoke drifted into my cubicle, and I sat very still, staring at the wall between us. *I must be misunderstanding*, I told myself. He couldn't be saying what I thought I was hearing. He couldn't be—

"... yeah, thirty-nine Gay Street ... the basement apartment, I said ... I'll meet you there ... right away ..." A threatening tone rose in the voice. "You better be there. If you're not it won't make any difference ... I'll be seeing you soon. Yeah, go downstairs to the basement apartment ... I'll be there. ..."

I heard the click of the receiver. I forgot all about telephoning for a telephone and made a dash for Jeff. I wanted to be someplace very close to him when that voice came out of its booth.

CHAPTER TWO

From our table we could see the phone booth, but not into it. Nobody could have emerged from it without our noticing. And nobody had come out.

"Perhaps he's making another call," Jeff suggested.

"Perhaps," I said.

Jeff looked at me and smiled. "Haila, you're shaking."

"You would be, too, if you'd heard his voice. It wasn't nice."

"Are you sure you didn't misunderstand him?"

"No! He's going to meet someone in our apartment!"

"Not a woman, I hope. We can't have that."

"Jeff, when you're inviting a friend to tea, you don't use the tone that man was using. And you don't borrow apartments from people you've never even met. Jeff, stop grinning! I *didn't* misunderstand! I'm *not* exaggerating! I—"

"Shh!"

The glass-topped door of the phone booth was folding slowly back. A man stepped out, dug both hands deep into his pockets, and let his eyes travel around the restaurant. I might only have imagined it, but they seemed to rest longest on us. Or perhaps it was because both Jeff and I were staring at him so intently.

"I could take him," Jeff whispered. "He can't weigh more than a hundred and thirty."

The man hunched his shoulders, pulled the collar of his coat up around

19

his short neck, and shoved the pearl-gray hat far back on his head. Ink-black hair grew too thick and too low on his forehead, and one drooping eyelid over the burning dark eye gave his swarthy face a pinched look. I would never forget that face and yet, looking away, I couldn't have described his nose or mouth.

Lowering his head, he started across the room toward the bar. As he passed our table he brushed against my coat that was hanging over an extra chair, and it fell to the floor. He made no move to pick it up, although he had to step over it to pass us.

"Hey!" Jeff said, starting to his feet.

I pulled him down quickly. "No, Jeff."

The man gave no indication that he had heard or even noticed. He was at the bar now, leaning heavily against it. The bartender slid a bottle toward him, followed it with a shot glass and a water chaser. The man poured his drink with unsteady fingers, slopping more on the shiny bar than in his glass.

"The guy's drunk," Jeff said.

"He didn't sound drunk," I said. "But he does look it. And even if he weren't, he's not the type I want dropping into my apartment of an evening."

"I hate to imagine what his friends are like. For instance, that one he's going to meet at our place."

"If that was a friend he was talking to, he isn't very nice to his friends."

"Haila, are you sure you heard correctly?" Jeff's attitude had changed since he had seen the object of my eavesdropping. The light bantering tone was gone now.

"He said thirty-nine Gay Street, Jeff. And twice he said the basement apartment. How could I have—"

"Thirty-Nine Gay Street," Jeff mused. "Thirty-Nine Gay—" He suddenly banged his fist down on the table and let out a yelp that made everyone in the restaurant jump, then turn and stare. Everyone, that is, but the man at the bar.

"Darling," I exclaimed, "what in heaven's name—"

"Haila, I've got it!"

"Got what?"

"Everything! Thirty-Nine Gay Street! Why it's so familiar, why I think I've lived there. Haila, I *have* lived there! It's Joe's!"

"Joe's?" I repeated stupidly.

"Sure, Joe's. The old speakeasy. You remember!"

"Uh-uh."

"No, you wouldn't. It was before your time." Jeff leaned back and sighed in loving memory. "Joe's! The happy, happy hours I've spent there. The hours, days, months—"

"Jeff," I said, trying to keep my voice steady, "do you mean to say that we live in an old speakeasy?"

"Yes. But not in *any* old speakeasy. *Joe's!*"

"We live in Joe's," I said dully. "A fine place to bring up children."

"Darling, you don't seem to realize what this means to me. It's like time slipping from my shoulders. It'll be reliving my salad days all over again. Why, it's like George Washington going back to Mount Vernon after—"

"Mount Vernon and Joe's! A couple of shrines. We're moving out tomorrow."

"Now, Haila, don't be cruel."

"We can break our lease."

"Haila, don't the scenes of my boyhood mean anything at all to you—"

I nudged him sharply and whispered, "Look!"

Our friend had left the bar and taken three or four steps back toward the phone booth. He hesitated and stopped. Then he returned to the bar, laying both his hands flat upon its top.

"Haila," Jeff said, "I can explain the whole thing to you now. That guy and his phone call."

"Please do."

"Joe's. The fellow's drunk, and his mind has slipped back. He thinks it's prohibition again. He wants somebody to meet him at his old speak."

"Hmm. Possibly."

"Sure, that's it. I don't remember him, but he's probably an old pal of mine."

"I can believe that."

"Haven't you ever got tight and thought it was ten years ago?"

"No."

"Well, how else would you explain that phone call?"

"Your way's as good as any," I admitted, but I was hardly satisfied.

"I bet I'm right. I'll see if I am. C'mon, let's talk to him."

"I'd rather not get involved—"

"Look, Haila, if we don't head him off, we'll have a drunk banging on our door all night."

Jeff started toward the bar, and I followed, keeping two good long steps behind. I wanted to hear, but I didn't care about meeting personally any minds that had just knocked a decade off the calendar, if such was the case.

Jeff clapped a friendly hand on the man's shoulder. The man wheeled around as if he had been bitten by a snake. But that didn't faze my husband, not *my* husband. In a voice that would have made Dale Carnegie wince with jealousy, he shouted, "Well, what d'ya know! Imagine meeting you here! It's been all of years! Years!"

The man regarded him icily. "I think you've got the wrong party, friend," he said, turning his back on Jeff and reaching for his nearly empty glass.

Jeff squeezed into a space beside him at the bar. "You don't remember me, huh? Joe's, you know, Joe's! Don't you remember now?"

The man didn't raise his eyes from the glass before him. "You've got the wrong party, friend," he repeated. He moved a foot or two down the bar, away from Jeff.

"We used to drink together at Joe's," Jeff persisted. "In the good old—"

The man slammed his open hand down on the bar and turned to glare at Jeff. "Leave me the hell alone," he said.

The bartender edged anxiously forward and hovered opposite Jeff and his nonremembering friend. But Jeff went blithely on.

"I want to do you a favor, that's all. Joe's is closed now. Get me? It's closed. I wouldn't bother going around there if I were you."

The man stepped toward Jeff, and the whole restaurant quieted to listen as his strangely hoarse voice cut gratingly through the room. "Listen, pal, it's no goddamn business of yours where I go or what—"

Jeff touched him restrainingly on the shoulder. "Keep it down to a shout, mister," he pleaded.

Mister viciously shrugged Jeff off and his right hand moved with sudden furtiveness to his right hip pocket. I stifled my warning scream as Jeff removed the necessity for it. Pushing the stranger tight against the bar, he pinioned his right arm between it and the man's own body.

The bartender vaulted across the bar and the little Filipino waiters danced hesitatingly around the outskirts of the fracas. The man, still in Jeff's body block, choked out harsh expletives that opened wide both the mouths and eyes of the female diners. Their escorts, stunned by danger, but goaded to action by immorality, rose and moved toward the bar.

Jeff was saying quietly to the man, "All I want you to remember is this. Stay away from Joe's tonight. Don't come around there or—"

"Or what?" The words were ground out between gritted teeth.

"Or else," Jeff said. "You know, else."

With an ugly scowl the man thrust Jeff away from him and slammed out of the restaurant. The bartender went back to polishing his glasses with an audible sigh of relief. The general conversation hummed up to a din again as the diners returned to their meals. I saw Polly Franklin, who had emerged from the kitchen at the tail end of the scene, speak briefly to a waiter and then disappear through a side exit.

Back at our table again, I steadied my shaking fingers on a water goblet, while Jeff rubbed his hand glumly across his eyes. "Dammit," he said.

"What's the matter?"

"I'm a heel. That guy wasn't bothering anyone, and I moved in with my big nose and bingo! Out he goes! He was just a harmless drunk."

"Harmless! He had a gun, didn't he?"

"He wasn't going to use it until I declared open season on myself. I'm a troublemaker, Haila. Disregard me."

"Well, anyway, he won't be pounding on our door tonight. Or singing 'Sweet Adeline' under our window."

Jeff laughed. "He'd better not. Or else! I'm glad he didn't ask me or else what. He'd have had me there."

"If he should show up, I know what'll happen."

"What?"

"You'll invite him in for a drink."

"He's probably a very nice guy."

"Probably. But he's not my type. And I hope his friend doesn't show up, either."

"His friend was yessing him to get him off the wire. C'mon, let's get out of here. How about a movie?"

"Oh, no. There's furniture coming and work to be done. Our old speak isn't fit to live in. C'mon, let's go to Joe's."

Jeff's eyes lit up like a Macy's window at Christmas. "Yeah, let's get back! I remember one night a fellow who had just previously been with a healthy and enthusiastic brunette in a short skirt became irate. And jealous of me. He threw a bottle in my direction. It barely missed and hit a doorframe. I bet the mark is still there. I'll show it to you."

"Oh, what fun! Looking at old bottle marks!"

"Haila, if I'd known you then, I'd have taken you to Joe's."

"You know me now, darling. And you can take me now. Oh, *do* let's go to Joe's! I want to take a bath and go to bed."

On our way to what only a few hours before I had thought of fondly as our new home, and not a retired saloon of doubtful repute, we did our marketing. Ingredients for breakfast. Light bulbs, yellow soap, scrub rags, shelf paper, Bab-O, Rinso, Chipso, this and that.

The street lights had snapped on, lighted windows threw yellow squares upon the pavements, and Gay Street looked cozy and friendly, like the World's Fair exhibit of the Street of the Nineties. Its narrowness and crookedness added to the quaint, old-fashioned atmosphere.

In front of number thirty-nine, I stepped out to the curb to look up at the house. With the darkness cloaking its grimy, soot-stained bricks and the crumbling stones of the chimneys, it looked pleasant and friendly, too, like the street it stood on. The top windows were black, but the two below were lighted and a child's face peered down at us from one of them. I smiled and started to wave. Then I caught myself.

The little face, pressed snub-nosed against the glass, was not a child's. It was a woman who was staring at us.

"Look, Jeff," I said, "we're being sized up."

He didn't see it. Before he could even raise his eyes a black-coated arm pulled the person away from the window and snapped down the shade.

Jeff was asking, "Where? I don't see anything."

"It's gone now."

"One of our neighbors being curious about the new tenants, huh?"

"Yes, I suppose so, but—it was staring so and it had a face that—"

"Don't you like your neighbors to have faces?" He took my arm and propelled me into the vestibule, then stopped abruptly in front of our apartment door. "Hey! No lock on our house!" He was right; where the

lock should have been, a round black hole gaped at us. "Did you notice
that before, Haila?"

"Um-hum, but I forgot to mention it," I admitted. "Me and Charley,
our memories."

"We'll see about it tomorrow."

We went through our lockless door and into our empty bedroom. By
the light of one of those low-watt bulbs found in vacant apartments, I
slipped out of my suit coat, armed myself with the scrub rags and soap
we had just purchased, and started for the bathroom. It was first on my
cleaning list.

"Hey, Haila!" Jeff's triumphant shout from the next room split the
air. "That bottle mark's still here!" I found him in front of a doorframe,
gazing at it with reverent awe. "Look, it's filed for posterity."

"Sorry," I said, "I'm busy."

I passed him and pulled open the bathroom door. I found the wall
switch and clicked it, not really expecting anything to happen. But our
accommodating landlord had left one of his midget bulbs in the ceiling
fixture there, too.

"Haila," Jeff called. There were practically tears in his voice. "You
can even see the marks on the floor where the bar stood. It was only a
little one, built around the fireplace. Some of my footprints should be
here. Why, one weekend I stood right on this spot for thirty-six con-
secutive hours. Without moving. I bet a guy I could do it without taking
a drink. I pocketed the money and fainted dead away. While I was out,
he stole back the money and left town. But, what the hell, it was only
two bucks—"

Jeff's voice went on, but I had stopped listening. I was staring unbe-
lievingly into the tub.

There was water running out of it.

"Jeff!"

He came hurrying into the bathroom. I pointed to the tub. We watched
a final rush of water, that last little swirl, go gurgling down the drain.

"What the—" Jeff said.

"Did you see what I saw?"

"Goldilocks!"

"What?"

"Who's been in our tub? Haila, maybe Charley's been cleaning
it."

"He couldn't have been. Look at it, it's still a mess. Besides, where is he, if—"

"Wait!" In a moment Jeff was back. "There's nobody in the kitchen. Or any place."

"But, Jeff, somebody was in here! Somebody filled the tub with water and then let it run out!"

"But who in—"

"Our friend at Polly's, maybe."

"He didn't look like the type of drunk who goes around bathing in strange tubs. Darling, don't get upset about it. Stop worrying; it's nothing."

"Nothing!" I wailed. "First the furniture is hours late! Then my new home turns out to be an old speakeasy of yours. Then a drunk makes dates here; then he nearly kills you. I see a ghoul's face leering out of the window at me and I find water running out of my bathtub and—"

"Now, Haila, everything's all right. I can explain it all."

"Well, go ahead. Don't just stand there."

"It's simple. The place is merely haunted."

"Oh, shut up! And, furthermore, my old pal Anne gives me the brush-off! That's what really rankles. What's the matter with us, anyway? Does she think we're going to keep goats in the garden or—"

The arrival of our furniture put an end to my tirade. The next hour was a nightmare of weary, straining men shuttling from the truck at the curb to the house, of barrels, boxes, crates, and trunks, of naked mattresses and dismembered furniture and rolled rugs bent double as if wracked with pain.

The moment the men had straggled off we found our bed, made it, and collapsed upon it.

If October first ever happened to come around again, I was going to be out to lunch. Jeff and I would spend the rest of our days at 39 Gay Street. I snuggled into my pillow, pulled the covers up to my chin, and pressed closer to Jeff.

"Haila."

His voice in the darkness was strangely perturbed.

"Yes?"

"That drunk over at Polly's—"

"What about him?" I asked, more than half asleep.

"He wasn't drunk," Jeff said slowly. "He was frightened. He was the most frightened human being I've ever seen."

CHAPTER THREE

AT FIRST I WASN'T QUITE SURE that I was awake. Having lived a reasonably sheltered life, I wasn't accustomed to having my day begin with a rattling din in my ears and a blinding light in my eyes. However, it was with gratitude that I identified the light; somehow the New York sun, adept by long experience at such gymnastic feats, had found a way to sneak into our nether apartment. I squinted through the glare toward the window, trying now to locate the noise. A big red fist was knocking at the glass.

"Jeff," I mumbled, "somebody wants in. In the window."

I reached out to shake him and my hand met the rumpled emptiness of his four-fifths of bed. The tattooing at the window rose to a threatening rumble and was joined by a pounding on the door. "All right, I'm coming," I yelled, and struggled, still foggy-brained, into my bathrobe and slippers.

It wasn't until I had pulled open the door and found myself face to face with a slew of brass buttons that I fully woke up. That wasn't soon enough. Before I could open my mouth or close the door, a mountainous policeman had pushed past me into my bedroom.

"Hey!" I said.

"You sure were asleep, miss!"

He strode to the window and made signals through it. "I'm in, Tom!"

he shouted. "You watch the front. Don't let no one out!"

"Hey!" I said again.

He brushed me aside and was disappearing into the dimness of our windowless middle room when I started after him. He turned back to me. His big blue bulk had no difficulty plugging the doorway.

"Not so quick, miss. Better wait in here."

"But what is it? What's happened?"

"Maybe nothing. That's what these hysterical biddies' reports usually amount to."

"But I didn't report anything."

"Lady upstairs did." He glanced over my head, behind me. "What about the front, Tom?"

"Man on the beat showed up. He's covering it."

Tom, a fellow minion of the law, was striding toward us across the bedroom. Combined, the two of them could have bottlenecked a modest canyon.

"Good," officer number one said. "You keep this here lady quiet in here. I'll take a look."

Tom took me gently by the arm and led me toward the bed. When our direction became obvious, he hastily changed course and landed me on a chair. "You sit down, lady. Please."

"Look, Tom," I said menacingly, "if this place is on fire and you let me burn to a crisp—"

"I wouldn't let you burn to a crisp," he said, offended. He was peering anxiously through the bedroom door, trying to see into the back of the apartment.

"What's happened?" I shouted.

"We'll know in a minute."

The sound of an approaching siren attracted my attention. A crowd had already gathered on the sidewalk. I could see the children from toe to tip. But because ours was a basement apartment, only the bottom half of the adults was within my range of vision. The man on the beat was trying to move them along, his mace swinging politely from his wrist. Through the gap he effected I could see the shiny body of a prowl car. The siren crescendoed and another prowl car swerved to a stop behind the first.

In a second, two more of the city's finest were coming through my bedroom door. They looked questioningly at Tom, but before either of them had time to speak, a voice came bellowing through the length of the apartment from the garden beyond.

"Tom!"

"Yeah?"

"Lady upstairs was right!"

"Stiff?"

"As a ramrod."

"Naked?"

"As a bluejay!" the voice responded heartily.

Then the panic that I had been fighting down broke loose inside me. I dived across the bed. Jeff's pajamas lay on the floor beside it in their usual tidy heap. My eyes flew to the chair in front of my dressing table. Over its back hung Jeff's gray suit, just as I had last seen it before closing my eyes the night before.

Somehow I managed to twist away from the policeman who tried to hold me, and somehow I managed to run. The middle room seemed like an endless tunnel as I raced through it; the two short steps up into the living room became a whole steep flight as I climbed them; the living room was the width of the Mississippi.

At last I stood in the garden in the bright, almost blinding sunshine. The policeman straightened up from his task of arranging newspapers over something that lay on the ground, and looked at me. People hanging out of back windows were looking at me. The concrete boy and concrete fish were looking at me. And I stood looking at the shapeless mass under the newspapers.

I moved over to the fountain beside which it lay, and lifted the paper. My eyes finally focused on an ear, then a head of hair. Thick, ink-black hair that grew too low on the brow. A face, swarthy and pinched-looking. One eyelid that, even in death, seemed to droop more than the other. A nose and mouth, both nondescript.

My teeth began to chatter, my knees to wobble. I felt a thick, reassuring arm come around my shoulders and a voice said, "You deserve it, miss; go ahead, faint." Before I had a chance to thank him, I did.

I was back in the living room, lying on two drawn-together easy chairs, when I came to. A short gentleman with small, penetrating eyes in a heavy face was waiting impatiently, waiting for me.

"I'm Hankins," he said, "of the homicide squad."

"Oh! Oh, then it is—"

"What else?"

I turned to look out the window. Quite a lot of time must have elapsed while I rested blissfully in my faint. The police photographer was already at work, focusing his camera on the corpse, the fountain, the fence, the yard, the house behind it. A lanky individual with a black satchel stood near by, waiting his turn. That would be the medical examiner. Two men in uniform were fine-combing every inch of Jeff's loam, while a fingerprint man blew powder on the French doors and casement windows.

Hankins moved in front of me, blocking my view.

"You're Mrs. Troy?" he asked.

"Yes," I said. I sat up.

"You better take it easy."

"I'm fine," I said, standing. I sat down quickly. "Well, as good as I should expect to be after finding a naked body in my garden before breakfast."

"Don't think about it."

I couldn't restrain a smile. "I can imagine your letting me forget about it, Mr. Hankins. How—how long has it been there?"

"We'll know exactly after the Medical Examiner makes his report. What's the use of guessing? Now, Mrs. Troy—"

"I don't know a thing about this! I wasn't even aware that anything was wrong until the police came banging on my door! Look, Mr. Hankins—"

"Take it easy, Mrs. Troy."

"Don't take-it-easy me! I don't need it. I'm not the hysterical type! That's the first time in all my life I ever fainted, and the only reason I did then was because I thought it was—" I couldn't seem to go on.

Hankins read my mind. "Where is your husband, Mrs. Troy?"

"What time is it?"

"Nine-thirty."

"Then he's at work. Photo Arts. It's in the Graylock Building."

Hankins nodded to a husky young man who lounged against the frame of the kitchen door. The husky started out of the apartment.

"Are—are you going to get Jeff?" I asked.

"Wouldn't you like him to be here?"

"I'd love it."

"So would we. Send a car for him, Bolling."

"Yeah."

"And find out what's holding up the landlord. I want to see him before I talk to the tenants."

"Okay."

With a quick, easy motion, Hankins grasped the back of my chair and swung it completely around so that I no longer faced the windows. He had also arranged that the morbidly curious among our neighbors were not being satisfied. Four of my best blankets were hanging on a clothesline stretched from fence to fence about ten feet behind the fountain.

"Who is he, Mrs. Troy?"

"I don't know."

"No?" The sandy eyebrows leaped in surprise.

"I suppose I should know. It being my garden. But I don't."

"The officer told me that you seemed to recognize him."

"Well, I—I *had* seen him before. But just once."

"When and where was that?"

"Last night, while we were having dinner. At Polly's. It's a little bit the other side of Seventh Avenue on Grove Street."

"I'd call that a strange coincidence, Mrs. Troy." He sat there silently, waiting for me to explain. I knew I'd have to, but I hesitated. It *was* a strange coincidence and my story would only make it stranger. "Go ahead, please, Mrs. Troy."

"Well, you see—" And I rattled off the whole crazy business, beginning with the voice in the phone booth next to mine and ending with the exit of the voice's owner from the restaurant.

The detective was frowning when I finished. "And you heard him tell someone to go *downstairs* and meet him. Is that right?"

"Yes. 'Go downstairs to the basement apartment—' I think those were his exact words."

"He was drunk, you say?"

"We thought at the time that he was. But later Jeff decided that he wasn't. That he was frightened, terribly frightened."

Hankins stepped into the garden, spoke softly to the Medical Examiner, who nodded blandly at him, and then came back to me.

"You're sure that this was the address the victim was giving over the phone in Polly's?"

"This address and this apartment."

"You have any idea who was on the other end of the line? Who he was talking to?"

"He didn't mention any names at all."

"Could you tell whether it was a man or a woman?"

"No."

"You're sure *he* made the arrangements to meet here? Not the other person?"

"He made the arrangements. Very definitely."

"The victim?"

"Yes."

That, it seemed, was food for thought and, mentally munching upon it, Hankins stared out the window at my maroon blanket, second from the left. After a minute or two, he turned to stare at me, much as if I, too, were a blanket, wet.

I felt that someone should say something. "Uh—have you found his clothing?"

"We've only been here fifteen minutes, Mrs. Troy," he answered testily. He swung around to face his assistant, Bolling, who had just lumbered in through the arch. "Where's the landlord?" he snapped.

"We haven't managed to locate him yet. I've sent two men looking for him."

"We can't wait any longer. Round up the tenants, Bolling. Send in the lady who reported this first."

It was Anne Carstairs who had notified the police. She was shaken and pale when she walked, hesitatingly, into our living room.

"Haila!" She ran across the room and took my hands in hers. "Haila, how awful this is for you. I'm so sorry that—"

"Lady!" Hankins had her by the arm, pulling her around to him. "I'm afraid that you'll have to talk to me first. Your name is Carstairs?"

She nodded. "Anne Carstairs."

"When did you see—" He jerked his head in the direction of the garden. "Tell me about it."

"It was after breakfast, after my husband had left for work. I happened to look out the window and I saw it. At first I couldn't tell what it was. I couldn't believe that—then I realized, and phoned the police. That's all I did."

"Which is your apartment?"

"The third floor. The whole floor."

"Counting this as the first?" Anne nodded, and Hankins went on. "Too high for you to get a good look at the victim. Would you mind going out into the garden now?"

Anne took a deep breath. "I have to, don't I?"

"I'm sorry, Mrs. Carstairs."

"All right. You needn't come with me."

When Anne came back, she sat on the arm of a love seat and squeezed both hands together to keep them from shaking. Hankins offered her a cigarette.

"No, thanks," she said.

"Well, Mrs. Carstairs?"

She raised her eyes to the detective and said, "That's Mr. Kaufman. He lives on the fifth floor."

"He lives here?" I gasped.

Hankins wheeled on me. "You didn't know that?"

"We only moved in yesterday afternoon!"

He turned back to Anne. "What's his first name?"

"I don't know. It's probably on the mailbox, but I never noticed."

"Did he live alone?"

"I don't know anything about him!" Anne was having trouble keeping herself under control. "I know his name's Kaufman. I know he lives in the back apartment of the top floor, as far as I know alone. I've seen him on the stairs. We said hello to each other. Never more than that."

"How long has he lived here?"

"He was here when Scott and I moved in last year. I don't know a thing about him."

"All right, Mrs. Carstairs. You better go and lie down. Stay in your apartment, I'll be wanting to talk to you again. What about your husband?"

"I phoned Scott. He should be here soon."

"You can go now. Thanks."

Anne looked at me as if there were a thousand things she wanted to say, but Hankins let her say none of them. Taking her firmly by the arm, he shepherded her out into the hall.

A moment later an elderly woman was being escorted in by a man some years younger than she. The lady's age, because of her lovely complexion and the sharpness of her eyes, was difficult to judge. She was probably in her sixties. Her hair, a shimmering white, was carefully arranged, and her keen blue eyes were heavily fringed with long lashes, still naturally black. She was stout, stout enough to be breathing laboriously from the walk to our apartment and through it. She sat down immediately and gratefully.

The gentleman was giving her all the moral support he could spare. He was about ten years younger than the woman, tall and slender and well dressed. His eyes were the kind that seem to smile no matter what their owner is doing or feeling. His thick brown hair was sprinkled with frosty gray.

Hankins was looking at him. "Your name?"

The man said, "Henry Lingle."

"And this is your wife." Hankins stated this as a matter of course.

"Oh, no," the lady said, with an attempt at a smile. I got the impression that at any other time she would have been flattered by the detective's conclusion. "I'm Miss Charlotte Griffith. I live with my sister."

The detective raised his eyebrows. "Why isn't your sister here? I want to see everyone."

Miss Griffith hesitated. "Lucy isn't—isn't well."

"Oh," Hankins said, softening a bit. "Did this business upset her or—"

"I don't think you understand. My sister is an invalid. It's impossible for her to leave her bed."

"I'll talk to her in your apartment," Hankins said, embarrassed by his own clumsiness.

"I'm afraid that—well, unless it's absolutely necessary, I wish you wouldn't. Please. I'm sure that Lucy wouldn't be of any help to you and it would just upset her more than—"

"I'll talk to you later about it, Miss Griffith," Hankins said. "Which floor are you and your sister living on?"

"We have all of the fourth floor."

I raised my head sharply, remembering. It had been at the fourth-floor window that I had seen the white, staring face. It had been the invalid sister, then, that I had caught watching us, the arm of this woman who had pulled down the blind. Miss Charlotte Griffith's story was true only in part. For, although that face had surely been the face of a sick woman, it had not been impossible for her to leave her bed last night.

"Mr. Lingle," Hankins was saying, "which is your apartment?"

"The one just above here. The back half of the floor."

Hankins said, "I'd like you and Miss Griffith to take a look at the victim."

"The victim," Lingle said. "Then it's murder?"

"I wouldn't be surprised," Hankins said sourly. "It's out there in the garden."

Miss Griffith glanced anxiously out through the French doors. "Oh, dear, I—"

"It'll just take a minute," Hankins said to her.

But, surprisingly, Mr. Lingle was more affected by the excursion to the corpse than Miss Griffith. She lumbered back to her seat, concerned mainly with the effort of navigation; his calmness was noticeably pierced. There was a slight twitching at the corners of his mouth, a trembling in the hands held rigidly at his sides.

Hankins noticed his agitation and pounced on him. "Well, Mr. Lingle?"

"His name is Kaufman, Michael Kaufman. He lived in one of the apartments on the top floor."

"Yes," Hankins said. "And what about him, Mr. Lingle? Where does he work? Where is his family?"

"I'm sorry. That's all I know about him."

"How long have you lived here?"

"Four years."

"And Kaufman? How long for him?"

"I believe he moved in the same time I did," Lingle answered.

"Four years ago? And in all those years you've never learned a thing about him?"

Lingle smiled uncertainly. "That happens in New York apartment houses. Even ones as small as this."

"So they say," Hankins said doubtfully and turned to Miss Griffith.

She anticipated his question and said, "I know nothing about him. I wouldn't even have known his name."

"You're new in this house?"

"My sister and I have been here just two years. And between my position at an employment agency and Lucy to care for, I haven't had much time to become acquainted with my neighbors. Not nearly so well acquainted as I would like to be."

With an annoyed grunt Hankins dismissed them both and went back into the garden for another conference with the Medical Examiner. Together they paced across the yard, pausing occasionally to bend over the corpse. By now the garden was jammed with police and the activity out there had increased. More plainclothes men had joined the ones already present, and the fence, the fountain, the back of our building, even the sumac tree, were being given a rigorous reinspection.

The assistant, Bolling, came stamping through the middle room, and Hankins stepped inside to meet him. "Have you located the landlord?"

"Not yet," Bolling answered. "So the victim lived here, huh? Top floor. Should I go up and look over his apartment?"

"Later. We'll do that after I've talked to everyone."

"Okay. There's a Miss Polly Franklin you haven't seen yet. She lives next to the victim, same floor."

"Send her in."

Miss Polly Franklin didn't need the raucous, colorful background of her restaurant to provide her with glamour. In the middle of the morning and a murder investigation it surrounded her. It would be there, too, in a Fourteenth Street dress shoppe bargain; at the Dublin Café on Eighth Avenue; in a bathing-suit at Coney Island or, as she was now, in a tweed skirt and a white sweater with the puzzling word *Hellions* in crimson across her bosom. The *el* and the *on* in the word were so provocatively raised, as if in triple Braille, that Hankins took to self-consciously studying his fingernails.

"Miss Franklin," he said, "would you mind taking a look at the victim?"

"Well—no. If he promises not to look at me."

Polly laughed, but there was nervousness and distaste and very little humor in it. When she came back into the living room, she was a trifle pale but not otherwise visibly affected.

"He's my next-door neighbor," she said. "His name's Mike Kaufman."

"Mike?" The detective's bright little eyes opened wide. "And did he call you Polly?"

"We never spoke to each other. But everyone referred to him as

Mike. You'd hardly call a character like that Michael. He was a sour puss if I ever saw one."

"Did he have any friends? Did anybody visit him?"

"Not that I know of."

"You lived next door, you'd know."

"I have a restaurant on Grove Street. Most of my time is spent there."

"Well, where did he work? What was he?"

Polly shrugged her wide shoulders.

"How long have you lived here, Miss Franklin?"

"Three years now."

"You've lived side by side for three years and you don't know anything about him?"

"That's exactly right, darling. I couldn't have worded it better myself."

The detective was momentarily stopped by the "darling." He couldn't tell if Polly was being coy or sarcastic. She was being neither. Her "darling" might just as well have been "Butch" or "you."

There were hurried steps in the middle room, and I turned just in time to see Jeff come through the arch. He looked at Hankins, smiled at me, and beamed from ear to ear at Polly Franklin.

Hankins growled, "Who are you?"

"I'm Jeff Troy!" my husband answered, and there was a good deal more pride in his voice than the simple statement warranted. "What's happened? Your man wouldn't tell me."

Hankins indicated the garden with a flip of his thumb. Jeff glanced through the windows at the teeming activity outside, then turned back to the detective.

"A murder," he said.

"And how," Hankins asked pointedly, "did you arrive at that conclusion so soon, Mr. Troy?"

"Easy. In the first place, a body. In the second, the homicide squad. And in the third place—and this is the clincher—Haila picked out this apartment."

CHAPTER FOUR

HAVING EXCUSED POLLY FRANKLIN, Hankins turned hastily to Jeff, intercepting him on his way to me. The detective seemed overly anxious to prevent any sort of family gathering.

"Troy!"

"Yes, sir?"

"I'd like you to take a look at the corpse." Before Jeff could even complete the questioning glance he tossed in my direction, Hankins had him by the arm. "It's in the garden."

Jeff accosted the body with much the same misgivings one has when sitting on a chair that has been heartily endorsed by a practical joker. He crouched down beside the remains of Mike Kaufman, his face out of my range of vision. When he finally arose his expression was dwindling to one of mere amazement. He came slowly back into the living room and, ignoring the detective, made a straight line for me.

"Haila—"

"Troy!" Hankins was visibly peeved. "You talk to me, will you? You recognized the victim, didn't you?"

"Yes."

"Tell me about him."

"Haila's told you."

"Yeah, but I want to hear it in your own words."

"Is it important that our versions be the same?" Jeff asked in a worried tone.

"Darling!" I said. "I told the truth! I told him everything I could remember!"

38

"I bet," Hankins said dryly, "that you two never lose at bridge. Go on, Troy, it's your lead."

Jeff went into much more detail in his account of the events at Polly's restaurant than I, in my weak and stunned condition, had been able to. But our stories, fortunately, were identical.

"When the victim left the restaurant," Hankins asked, "did he head in this direction?"

"I couldn't tell you. I didn't see him to the door. And I didn't see him again until just now."

"No?"

"No," Jeff said emphatically. Hankins nodded in complete acceptance. But the completeness went too far. It ended by being perfunctory and, therefore, more than a little disconcerting. But before either Jeff's or my reaction could crystallize into word or deed, a voice had come through the archway.

"I'm Scott Carstairs."

At first sight I recognized him as the man Anne had been dreaming about ever since she was a little girl. Scott Carstairs had the kind of good looks that could have made him a matinee idol and yet keep him unsneered at by the other members of his sex. He was handsome and would probably have torn anyone into shreds who accused him of such a thing. His crisply curling blond hair and vivid-blue eyes seemed to emphasize the grimness of his mouth as he approached Hankins now.

"One of your men sent me in here," he said. "Can't I see my wife a minute before—"

"You can see her later."

"I'd like to make sure she's all right!"

"She's fine," Hankins told him. "Now go out there and see if you can identify the corpse, Mr. Carstairs."

We watched Anne's husband make the same unpleasant pilgrimage that all his predecessors had been forced to make. When he came back he said in puzzled surprise, "That's Mike Kaufman. He lives upstairs—the top floor."

Jeff jumped to his feet. "He lives here?"

"And that's news to you, huh, Troy?" Hankins's voice insinuated the reverse.

"Well, of course! How would I know that?"

Hankins had turned back to Scott. "What do you know about this Kaufman, Carstairs?"

"Not a thing. I know his name, I know where he lived. That's all. I never spoke to the man in my life."

Hankins grunted. "All right, you can go now. But stick around. I'll be up to have a talk with you and your wife later."

Without even a glance at Jeff or me, Scott Carstairs hurried away. Hankins moved over to the French doors and called to the group of men who surrounded the medical examiner and the object of his examination. For the past ten minutes they had been chatting socially, smoking, leaning, sitting, obviously awaiting further orders.

"Take him away, boys," Hankins commanded.

Two of the boys rolled the body onto a stretcher and covered it with a canvas sheet. They lifted it and carried it into the living room, through the arch, down the two steps, and out through the middle room. This was one occasion to which the hostess in me made no attempt to rise; this was one guest whose departure I didn't have to protest. I merely covered my eyes with both hands and waited until I heard the bell of the police ambulance fade away in the distance.

Hankins conferred for a moment or two in the middle room with his aide, Bolling. Then he came back to us, carefully chose a straight-backed chair, planted one foot on it, and leaned across his knee toward us.

"Troy," he said thoughtfully. "Jeff Troy. Where have I heard that name before?"

"Were you at Madison Square Garden the night my name was announced over the public-address system? Haila was locked out and she wanted my key. Is how Kaufman was killed a secret?"

"Oh, yeah!" Hankins said. "You're an amateur dick! You solved that theater murder—and that killing in the photographic studio. At least you got the credit for solving them."

"I didn't take the credit," Jeff said modestly. "I don't want to be a detective. All I want is to earn an honest living for my beautiful wife and self."

"Do you think you'll have any trouble solving this case, Troy?" There was more than a hint of mockery in the detective's voice.

"It's too early to tell. But you can't blame me for being interested when a murder goes right off in our faces."

"No, I can't. It's an interesting coincidence. But since you're a detective yourself, Troy, you won't mind if I ask you a few questions."

"Certainly not. Go right ahead. There was a bruise and a little cut behind Kaufman's right ear. But they couldn't have been responsible for his death. And I didn't see any bullet wound. So what did kill him?"

It took Hankins a moment to decide not to be annoyed. "Okay, Troy, I'll tell you how the victim died."

"I'd appreciate it."

"He was drowned."

"He was—what?" I stammered.

"Drowned!" Jeff said. "Drowned on dry land!"

"I doubt that," Hankins said.

"It didn't rain last night," Jeff rattled on, his logic knocked silly by bewilderment. "There isn't any water in the fountain, he couldn't have been delivered here from the Hudson River—or could he? Or what?"

"Jeff! Last night when we came home—the bathtub!"

"That's right, Mrs. Troy," Hankins said. "He was drowned in your tub. We found some of his hair caught in the drain. And what about last night when you came home?"

"There was water running out of our tub. Only a little was left, but it must have been filled to—"

"Yes!" Jeff said. "That bruise and cut behind Kaufman's ear. He must have been knocked out, dragged into the bathroom, and put in the tub. But!"

"But what, Troy?"

"Why drowned? Why not shot—with his own gun, even—or knifed or beaten to death?"

"Well," Hankins began, "perhaps—"

"If you don't mind, Mr. Hankins, I'll answer my own questions. A shot would have been heard by the people upstairs. The silent methods—well, why do people drown kittens? Because it's the least bloody, least violent, least unpleasant way of getting rid of something you don't want around. Strangling an already unconscious man would be—"

"Ugh!" I said, and shuddered accordingly.

"Highly ugh," Jeff agreed. "It takes a strong stomach to strangle something that offers no resistance—and this murderer obviously wasn't strong enough."

"So," Hankins said, "we should look for a man with a weak stomach, huh?"

"Well, it might be a clue to the killer's character, mightn't it? And another thing. A thing which I don't like. The method proves that the murder was committed in our apartment."

"That's been established. Your tub, your apartment, your garden."

"Maybe the murderer wanted that fact established," Jeff said.

"Maybe. Mrs. Troy, what time was it when you saw the water running out of your tub?"

"Between nine and nine-fifteen."

"And that establishes pretty well the time of the crime. The killer must have pulled the plug out of the tub only a few minutes before you arrived. Or say you arrived."

Jeff grinned at him. "But you'll take our word for that, won't you? Look, Hankins, the murderer must have dragged the body into the yard so that it would escape discovery as long as possible. But why did he strip it? Have you found any of his clothes?"

"No," Hankins said sourly.

Bolling shouted to his superior from the bedroom door. "I've located the landlord, he's out here now. Want to see him?"

"Send him in."

George Turner, having been ushered in by the burly Bolling, stood in the middle of the room and looked nervously and apologetically about him. He was a little man, his hands and feet so small that they seemed almost feminine. His eyes were meek and colorless, his face had the look of a scared rabbit. Never in a million years should George Turner have been cast as a landlord. If he could foreclose a mortgage, I could play tackle for West Point.

It seemed for a moment, when the detective moved toward him, that he would turn and run. But finally his head came up with a defiant thrust and he held his ground.

"It took you a long time to get here, Turner," Hankins said.

"I was—getting a haircut."

"Helluva time to be getting a haircut."

"I didn't know what—what had happened here until just now or I—"

"George Turner," the detective said slowly. He had been gazing down at the little man with narrowing eyes. "Turner, thirty-nine Gay Street.

The same name, the same address. I should have known. So you're still running this place."

"I still own this building," Turner said, his tone pleadingly corrective. Then his eyes lighted on me, and his decision to use his new tenants as an escape from Hankins was obvious. "I didn't expect you till next week, Mrs. Troy," he said reprovingly. "You should have let me know."

"It was Charley who should have let you know," I said. "I told him—"

Hankins stopped me. "Turner," he said sharply, "this time you're going to cooperate. With the police, I mean. Won't you, Turner?"

"I don't know what you're talking about. You ask me any questions you want and I'll tell the truth."

A quick ironic smile crossed Hankins's lips. "All right," he said, "we'll see. Who was Mike Kaufman?"

"A tenant of mine. Top floor, rear."

"How long's he lived here? What does he do? Where's his family?"

"Mr. Kaufman's been here four years now," Turner said, and promptly floundered.

"Go on."

"That's—that's all I know about him."

"What? Before you let him sign a lease, you checked up on him, didn't you? His employment, his bank account, his references?"

"No. A little two-room apartment, only forty a month. And he paid for two months in advance, I remember. I never checked up on him."

"In four years you must have found out *something* about him," Hankins insisted.

Turner shook his head. "Once a month he handed me his rent, that's all."

"Check or cash?"

"Cash."

"Where's the key to his apartment? We'll find out about him."

"I don't have a key to none of the apartments," Turner said. "It's better that way."

"It won't be better for the door to Kaufman's place," Hankins said grimly. He stood quietly for a long moment before his thoughts finally broke into words. "The Troys, the Carstairses, Miss Franklin, Lingle, Miss Griffith and her sister, and you, Turner. Leaving out the Troys, that's seven. Kaufman's murderer is one of those seven people."

Turner's gasp was clearly audible. "You mean that one of us—No, that's wrong! I'll show you! There's no lock on this apartment—it's being fixed now, and the street door is always open. Anyone could have come in here and—"

Hankins was emphatically shaking his head. "One of you seven, I said. And I'll show *you!* Mrs. Troy overheard Kaufman making a phone call just before his death. He told someone to go downstairs and meet him in the basement of thirty-nine Gay Street. Go *downstairs!* Get that? He was talking to somebody in this building. One of you is lying about not knowing Kaufman. One of you knows him very well. And that one is the killer."

"No," George Turner said, "no, you're wrong. All my tenants are fine people, they wouldn't—"

"All right, Turner," Hankins snapped impatiently, "you can run along now. And stay at home; I'll be dropping in."

We watched the landlord scamper gratefully away. Hankins turned to us, opened his mouth to speak, then changed his mind. "Bolling," he said, "we'll go through Kaufman's things now. And I bet we find out which one of these good people has been lying about knowing Mike Kaufman."

Jeff and I followed the two policemen up the stairs, tentatively at first, but when neither of them seemed to mind, we gathered speed and courage. We were right at their heels when they reached the top landing.

Hankins gave the knob of Kaufman's door a perfunctory rattle and push, then stepped aside. "Okay, Bolling, give it the works. My neuritis is bothering me."

Bolling braced one foot against the door, squared his mammoth shoulders, turned them sidewise, and lunged. There was a shattering sound and the door bounced wide open.

Not one of us moved or spoke. We stood staring at the apartment before us. At last Hankins emitted a grunt of amazement and walked through the doorway. We followed him.

Kaufman's was a two-room apartment. Unless you counted the makeshift kitchenette in the alcove and the bath. The doors into the one small bedroom, the shallow closet, and the bath were standing ajar. From where we stood we could view the entire apartment. And it was completely bare.

There was nothing in the place; not a stick of furniture, a picture, a curtain, a scrap of paper nor a hank of hair. Mike Kaufman's apartment was as clean as the proverbial whistle.

CHAPTER FIVE

"WELL, FOR—"

That exclamation of surprise came from behind us, and we turned to see Polly Franklin in the doorway, staring wide-eyed, open-mouthed into the room. Hankins stepped past Jeff and me to her.

"Is this the right apartment? Is this where Kaufman lived?"

She nodded, her face still blank with astonishment.

"When did he move his stuff out?" Hankins demanded.

"I'd have told you about it if I'd known he had. I'm not always around. Ask Turner; he'd know."

"Bolling, get Turner up here. And that janitor."

"Right!"

The assistant detective clumped out of the room and down the stairs. His boss stood and scowled at the barren apartment.

"An important thing like this," he said, "you'd think anybody in the building who knew about Kaufman moving, would have told me. But nobody did. And how the hell could two rooms of furniture get moved out without anybody noticing it? Miss Franklin, you're sure this place *was* furnished?"

"Well, the man lived here!"

"You've been in this apartment, you've visited Kaufman?"

"Listen, darling," Polly said with smiling impatience, "I told you before that Mike Kaufman and I didn't even talk about the weather to each other. But I've passed by when his door was open."

"And you saw furniture," Jeff said.

"Yes. And furthermore, the man wore clothes, he slept here, he ate here, he smoked and drank. I've seen empty bottles outside his door, I've smelled coffee cooking, I've heard his radio. Of course the place was furnished. He lived here! For over three years!"

"When did you see him last?" Jeff asked. "Alive I mean."

"Why—yesterday afternoon, darling. I didn't exactly see him, but I heard him come in about five o'clock. He turned on his radio to listen to the racing results."

Hankins opened his mouth, but Jeff, oblivious, enthusiastically continued his questioning. "Are you sure it was Kaufman's radio?"

"Positive. The only other apartment I can hear anything in is the Griffiths'. And they don't have a radio. Miss Charlotte was always complaining about the way Kaufman's blared. She hates radios."

"Then the furniture must have gone out of here since five o'clock yesterday afternoon—"

Hankins interrupted him in an icy drawl. "If you don't mind, Troy, I'd like to ask Miss Franklin some questions. If she has any answers left."

"I'm just trying to help," Jeff said. "Help speed justice."

"What do you think I get paid for?" Hankins demanded.

"If I answered that honestly, you'd arrest me."

Polly laughed, a deep-throated, all-out laugh. Hankins's face turned a dull red, but he kept his temper. For which I admired him. "Troy," he said, "you and your wife wait in your apartment. I'll see you later."

I took Jeff by the arm and marched him down the stairs. "Darling," I said, "it's wrong of you to get Hankins sore at you. Remember the body was found in our garden. We're as much suspects as anybody."

"New York's got some of the most brilliant detectives in the world on its homicide squad. Why did they have to send a lug like Hankins?"

"Why is he a lug?"

"He's too slow! Waiting so long before he discovered Kaufman's apartment was empty."

"Bolling wanted to go up an hour ago," I remembered.

"Sure," Jeff said, "but Hankins has to be the leading man, the star."

"You weren't doing so bad yourself upstairs, dear."

"I know and I'm sorry. But Haila!" He pulled me to a stop in front of our door. "I have a hunch this case has to be solved fast! I don't know why, but I can feel it hardening, settling down into a crack-proof crime."

"Which Hankins won't solve but you will," I snapped.

"I could break my arm for not learning more from the homicide bureau men on those other two murders."

"Darling, you found the murderer before they did each time!"

Jeff laughed at me. "You're on my side again, aren't you? That was luck, Haila. But this killer isn't going to be caught by luck." He stopped. "I wouldn't be surprised if he were listening to us right now."

"Maybe. He lives in this house. Let's go in." I took Jeff by the hand and led him into our apartment. One look at our domicile brought me to a decision. "Jeff, couldn't we just take an hour or two off from murder and try to make this place look like home? It would do wonders for my morale."

"Sure, tell me what to do."

I should have known; Jeff wasn't much help. He would pick up a lamp or a chair, walk thoughtfully around the room with it, then deposit it in exactly the same spot where it had been standing. Nevertheless, I was determined that if any more persons dropped in on us to be sprung from this mortal coil, they wouldn't find our house in such a mess.

I pulled, shoved, and coaxed furniture and Jeff into strategic places around the apartment until I was ready to drop. But finally, by practically resorting to hypnotism, I succeeded in making him do the last job; put a wedding present from one of his aunts way back on a top shelf where we couldn't see it. It was a lovely set of antimacassars.

Then I made a tour of inspection. The bedroom would do for the nonce, except for the windows. They needed shades, Venetian blinds, something. I didn't want the murder-hungry crowd outside on Gay Street to watch the corpse's hostess fluttering here and there in the pursuit of the mundane duties of a housewife. That would ruin my glamour for them. Then also I would be wanting to dress and vice versa here, and seeing me in that operation would surely destroy any stray glamour that might remain.

The middle room I ignored. That would take inspiration to make habitable. But the living room looked all right. Very.

Our love seats needed that big stone fireplace at the end of the room to hold them just close enough together for the leather-topped coffee table between to be easily accessible. Our books filled the shelves on either side of the fireplace without looking either crowded or lost. The flat-topped desk belonged right under the large casement window and the Duncan Phyffe table might have been designed to fit that wall space beside the kitchen door.

The late-afternoon sun flooding the room made me realize that, in some accidental way, we had achieved a color scheme, a kind of tawny brown and dusky blue with splotches of vivid yellow. In fact, if you could manage to keep your eyes from the windows and the patch of yard beyond them, it seemed a very lovely room indeed.

And even the garden didn't seem quite so grim at this point. Perhaps only by comparison. Now it was empty, no longer filled with an undecorative body and a bunch of not much more decorative police-men, photographers, fingerprint men, and so forth. Except for the nu-merous cigarette butts defiling the innocence of our little concrete boy and his friend the fish, there was no evidence of this morning's unpleas-antness. Even the neighbors' windows, which had been crammed with gaping people, were closed and shaded now as if, the drama being over, each individual curtain had been drawn upon the stage of it.

Each curtain except ours, that was. No matter how I tried, my eyes kept peeking back to that spot where I had envisioned daffodils, not naked corpses springing up.

Jeff came wandering restlessly into the living room. "I wish Hankins would hurry up and appear."

"He'll be here too soon to suit me. Jeff, please be polite. Let Hankins ask a few questions."

He wasn't even listening to me. "How in hell," he mused, "did the murderer get the furniture and everything else out of Kaufman's apart-ment without it being seen leaving the house?"

"Maybe the murderer didn't get it out," I suggested. "Kaufman could have taken it out himself, couldn't he?"

"Yes, but I don't think he did. Did you notice that apartment? It was cleaned out so thoroughly that you can't tell who—or even if anyone—ever lived there. Not an old razor blade, a magazine, a laundry list."

"Jeff, why would anybody go to all that trouble and risk?"

"For the same reason that he stripped the body. To prevent identifi-cation of the victim."

"But, for heaven's sake, he has been identified! His name is Mike Kaufman, he lived on the top floor of thirty-nine Gay Street, he—"

"Go on, Haila."

"Go on?"

"Sure, where did he work, where did he come from, who are his friends and his family? No one in this building can answer those questions. And how are the police going to find someone who can?"

"There are ways. It may take time, but nobody gets born in this country without there being a record. Birth certificates, public school records, driving licenses, and all that."

Jeff was shaking his head. "No. If the murderer thought that Mike Kaufman could be traced that way, he wouldn't have stripped his body and apartment. I bet the name Mike Kaufman won't be in any records. Because I bet there is no Mike Kaufman."

"But—"

"It has to be an alias, Haila. Or why would the murderer have stripped—"

"Yes," I admitted. "I can see that."

"Mike Kaufman's real identity," Jeff went on, "would establish a relationship between him and someone in this building. And that someone is the murderer. So the murderer obliterated Kaufman's real identity and any possibility of tracing it."

"I think you're right, Jeff. Then the killer cleaned out Kaufman's apartment."

"Sure, that and his body being stripped are part of the same maneuver. And Kaufman certainly didn't undress himself after he was dead. But how and when did that furniture leave his place?"

"I think I can help you on the when," I said slowly. "If Polly Franklin was right about hearing his radio around five o'clock yesterday afternoon—"

"Then his stuff was still there at five, yes."

"I got here a little before five, and you and I didn't leave for dinner until almost seven. Jeff, I'm sure that furniture couldn't have come down those stairs during that time without my being aware of it."

"I'm sure, too."

"And a half hour after we left here, we saw Kaufman in Polly's restaurant. He couldn't have done it in that short a time. So there's your clincher that the murderer moved the furniture, if you need one."

"Thanks," Jeff said. He stood looking at me without seeing me. "That means the furniture was moved out after the murder, during the night. While we were sleeping ten feet from the foot of the stairs."

"That's a thick wall, we mightn't have heard it."

"I mightn't have, but you would. When a pin drops over in Jersey, you wake up and ask me if I heard an explosion in our kitchen. That furniture—that furniture—" Jeff drummed out the rhythm on the top of our desk. "Kaufman's furniture and his clothes hold the secret. The clothes could have been ghosted away easily enough, but not two rooms of furniture. Not without anyone noticing it. You can't put furniture between two slices of bread and—"

"Oh, stop saying furniture! I'm filthy and I'm going to take a bath." I stood up. I sat down. "No. I'm not."

"Why?"

"I'm never going to take a bath. Not in *that* tub. I'll never set foot in it as long as I live."

"Oh, I see. But listen, Haila. The murderer probably just bent him over the edge and held his head under water. And he was unconscious all the time."

"That doesn't help!"

"But you'll have to take a bath *sometime!* Your background and your fear of public opinion—"

"Not in that tub. I'll join the Y.W."

"My wife," Jeff said in disgust, "is a sissy. I'll never be able to face my gang again—"

"You need a bath!"

"I?" Jeff was hurt.

"Sure you do. Go ahead and take one."

"I had a shower at the studio this morning."

"That's a lie."

"All right, it's a lie. But I don't need a bath."

"My husband is a sissy! I'll never be able to face the girls—"

"You dare me to take a bath?" Jeff shouted, sticking out his chin.

"You bet I do!"

He smiled at me with withering scorn. "Very well. I accept your challenge. I shall bathe." He kissed me formally on the forehead. "Excuse me, Haila. If anybody wants me, I shall be in the tub."

Quietly humming the "Marseillaise," he marched into the bathroom and slammed the door. The water roared as it churned into the tub. Jeff's voice rose above it in a medley of the French National Anthem, excerpts from *The Vagabond King*, the Notre Dame fight song, "Lover

Come Back to Me" and "Onward, Christian Soldiers." When he ran out of words, he changed his tune.

Eventually the roar of the water subsided. "Ouch!" Jeff shouted in acute agony. "Too damn hot! Ouch, ouch, ouch—a-a-a-ah!" Then a symphony of splashing and happy humming.

I began to really feel like a sissy. I went to the bathroom door and knocked on it.

"Jeff, when you finish, I'll take—"

"Don't come in!" he shouted. "Don't come in!"

There was too much fear and panic in his pleading. After all, we *were* married. I opened the door.

My fine husband stood beside the tub, fully dressed. With one hand he slashed at the water with a long-handled plunger, with the other he sprinkled water on a bath towel. He didn't see me.

"Boy, Haila!" he was shouting. "This is fine! First tub I can stretch full length in since I got my full growth!"

"My hero!"

He wheeled around. "Of all the sneaking, spying, sniveling—"

"You fraud! You deceitful—There's only one thing that can save our marriage now!"

"What?" Jeff asked sulkily.

"Vindicate yourself! Get in that tub!"

"Aw, Haila, it isn't that somebody was murdered in it—that doesn't bother me. It's just—just that I happened to remember—"

"Remember what?" I snapped.

"Joe used to make his gin in this tub."

"I suppose that's worse than a man being drowned in it!"

"You never tasted Joe's gin."

A series of sharp knocks bounced off our front door.

"I'll answer it," Jeff said, and rushed out.

I followed him, watched him open the door, and saw the two detectives walk in. Hankins was in a bad humor. Without a word, he stamped through the entire apartment, examining everything.

"Can you prove this is your furniture?" he asked at last.

"Prove it's ours?" I echoed in amazement.

"Oh," Jeff said, "so you think, too, that Kaufman's stuff never left this house?"

"It couldn't have!" Hankins shouted. "Somebody would have had to notice it, and no one did! I've searched the whole building and haven't found it. Can you prove this is your furniture?"

"Nice thinking," Jeff said. "Haila and I arrived here empty-handed. We spirited Mike Kaufman's furniture down the stairs and are now pretending that it's ours. But you're wrong."

"That's possible," Hankins admitted, but too reluctantly.

"Mr. Hankins," Jeff said, "don't forget that you eliminated Haila and me yourself. Because Kaufman told somebody to come downstairs."

"I made a mistake, Troy, I believed you. But I can't believe a word you or your wife say anymore."

"Huh?"

"You lied to me. I just got the report from one of my men. He talked to the bartender at Miss Franklin's restaurant. Troy, you did know Kaufman. The bartender says that when you approached Kaufman, you greeted him like a long lost friend."

"That's right, but—"

"When he didn't recognize you, you reminded him of how you used to drink together here in this place when it was a speak."

"Yes, but—"

"Then Kaufman seemed to remember—remember something that made him try to pull a gun on you! Why did he want to kill you, Troy? Certainly not because you were an old *friend* of his."

"I never saw Kaufman before last night!"

"You never saw Kaufman before! You accost a total stranger, you threaten him, you warn him not to do something or other—the bartender overheard that, too—and then this total stranger, this man you never saw before, tries to shoot you. Oh, no! You knew Kaufman, you knew him well enough to—"

"Listen!" Jeff bawled. "I thought he was drunk! I thought in his state he was under the impression our apartment was still Joe's and that he was going to meet someone here. I was only trying to head him off. I pulled that 'old pal' line to humor him, the way you do a drunk."

"He wasn't drunk! You told your wife that he wasn't drunk."

"That was later. At the time I thought he was plastered!"

"C'mon, Troy, tell me about Kaufman."

"I never saw him before last night," Jeff said wearily.

There was a long pause while Hankins eyed Jeff. Then the detective said, "What's the name of the company that moved you?"

"The Grayvan Lines," I answered.

"Check on it," Jeff said. "They'll prove they brought this stuff down from Connecticut. You know, Mr. Hankins, maybe Kaufman's furniture did leave the house, after all. He would have needed a truck—"

"I'm checking with every trucking and moving company within a hundred miles of here. Just to prove that the stuff is still in this house."

"I think it has to be," Jeff agreed. "Listen, does anyone have an alibi for the time of the murder? Can you eliminate anyone that way?"

Hankins grunted. "The time of the murder, alibis! First I've got to believe you two to set the time of the crime exactly, the time you say you saw the water running out of your tub. But accepting that, I checked on alibis. There isn't one in the house that's worth a damn. Nobody can prove that they couldn't have killed Kaufman."

"How about Jeff and me?" I demanded. "If we saw Kaufman make that phone call, we couldn't be the party he called."

"That's right," Hankins said. "You're the only people in the house with an alibi. Strange."

"I see," I said. "That telephone business could have been something clever we thought up."

"Sure," Jeff said grimly. "Look, Mr. Hankins, if it's wrong to have an alibi, we don't. We're lying about the phone call. We left Polly's in time to get here and kill Kaufman. Does that eliminate us?"

"It's very, very strange," Hankins drawled with maddening casualness. "Kaufman, not drunk, but frightened, makes a date to meet someone in your place. You threaten him; he tries to kill you. But you never saw him before. He has a gun, but he is drowned in your bathtub. His body is left in your yard. Troy, I was too hasty. When the fingerprint man was here, I didn't have him get yours. Suppose we go down to headquarters, shall we?"

"You don't have to take me down to headquarters just for my fingerprints," Jeff said uneasily.

"No, I don't," Hankins said. "So there must be other reasons. For instance, it's funny how people start telling the truth down in that neighborhood. Offer Troy your arm, Bolling."

CHAPTER SIX

FROM THE FRONT SEAT of the homicide squad car Jeff blew me a kiss. I had the unpleasant impression at that moment that he looked like Marie Antoinette. I had never noticed it before. And I fervently hoped that I never would again.

I wandered restlessly about the apartment wondering what a wife is supposed to do while her husband is being beaten with rubber hoses, stuck with pins, blinded by strong lights. When I reached the point where Hankins was shoving bamboo splits under Jeff's fingernails and lighting the bamboo, I shook myself. "Now, Haila," I said, "Mr. Hankins is not a fiend. He wouldn't hurt a fly, not really. He—"

But Jeff wasn't a fly, he—No, I had to stop this mental driveling. I would busy myself about our new home. The devil makes work for idle minds.

For two solid hours I scrubbed, dusted, arranged, and rearranged. I plunged from room to room like a berserk charwoman, never pausing for a cigarette or even a breath. And never for one second did I stop thinking, worrying, moping about my husband.

The apartment looked spick and span and wonderful. It was the kind of place I had dreamed of all my life. But I vowed by all the gods in all mythology that once this year was up we would move back uptown into one room, without bath, without garden and, consequently, without a corpse. The way I could do without a corpse!

By four o'clock there was still no sign of Jeff. I spent the next half hour shuttling between the door and the clock. I looked out the front windows and then out the back. I stared into the garden for so long that I thought I saw the fish leap from the boy's concrete arms and dive jubilantly into the water, wagging its tail behind it. I tried reading and then, with that disposed of, I worked on the radio for a while. I decided, after having found myself listening exclusively to police calls, that what I needed was someone to talk to. Someone who would sit quietly by my side, pat my hand reassuringly, and tell me that Jeff was on his way home.

I combed my hair, powdered my nose, and started through the apartment on my way to Anne Carstairs's. Just then I heard footsteps in the hall outside and, thinking it might be Anne paying me a visit, I ran through the bedroom and out into the hall.

It was empty. There was no one going up the stairs or coming down them. There was no one outside the front door. But someone had certainly been in that hall just a moment before. Puzzled, I meandered back down the length of it.

The light that filtered through the street entrance petered out long before it reached the depths of the narrow corridor, and it was pitch-black there. I reached out my hand to feel my way around and it touched a door knob.

I turned it and pulled. Below me stretched a flight of stairs that were dimly illuminated by a light somewhere in the basement. I could hear footsteps, slow shuffling ones, on the concrete floor beneath.

I closed the door and started up to the second floor, realizing that no disappearing act had been going on, after all. Murder or no murder, there were chores to be done about an apartment house, and Janitor Charley was doing them. And Charley's shoulder was definitely not the one I wished to dampen with my worried wifely tears.

I was already on the second landing when I heard him come up and stump through the hallway and, as he swung open the outside door, I saw him. I stopped dead in my tracks and stared.

Unless Charley had grown two full feet since the last time I had seen him, he had not been the man in our cellar.

The man who was not Charley hesitated for a moment at the entrance and then, apparently scrapping his plan for departure, retraced his steps to the basement. I had glimpsed his face as he passed beneath my watching-post. A beaklike nose, pinched by small, beady eyes that were too close together. A neck that was long and skinny and red. Long arms that dangled from narrow shoulders. All in all, hardly the type of fellow a girl invited to her junior prom.

It was the state I was in that made me do it. Ordinarily, when I hear footsteps in hallways, I disregard them. And ordinarily, when I see a Frankenstein descend into a cellar, I don't follow him. But at that moment I found myself suddenly overwhelmed with a desire to know why a stranger of that ilk should be prowling around in the bowels of our building.

I stopped, however, at the head of the cellar steps and listened. Down below, in what seemed to be a far corner, there was a clumping, bumping, pounding noise.

I sneaked very cautiously down the stairs. At the bottom I could still see nothing of the man himself. But I could hear him at his work somewhere beyond the crisscross of stone walls and wooden partitions that made the place a catacomb.

At last the thumping stopped and its place was taken by slow, dragging footsteps. Dragging in my direction. I slipped into the space beneath the stairs and wedged myself tight between two trunks that stood against the wall. From there I watched a pair of long legs and a shovel pass, all three being part or parcel of the male animal I was stalking.

He started up the stairs. I could feel his foot land on the tread my head was touching. And there it halted.

I hadn't made a sound; I was positive of that. But perhaps, with that voluminous nose of his, he had sniffed the *Tweed* which I had tucked behind each ear in an unconscious attempt to lure my husband—by long distance—home from the police. I shut my eyes and prayed that this gentleman was also allure-proof, that *Tweed* held no come-hither power for him. Or his shovel.

There was a scratching noise, and a moment later a kitchen match landed on the floor a foot in front of me. It kept on burning. Then the smell of cheap pipe tobacco rent the air, making my *Tweed* cower behind my ears.

The man resumed his ascent. He snapped off the lights, shut the door, and I heard the sharp click of the lock. The match before me sputtered and gave up the ghost, as if admitting its inadequacy to bear the burden of illumination alone.

After a long minute I groped my way up the stairs, only to make a pair of discouraging discoveries. The cellar door was the old-fashioned type that needed a key to open it from either side. And the light switch, as is often the case for cellars, was outside in the corridor.

I sat down on the top step, patted myself on the back with one hand, and awarded myself a cigarette with the other. I deserved a great deal more. I had done a thing which very few adults are able to manage; I had got myself locked in a cellar. A pitch-black cellar. My husband would be proud of me.

Nevertheless, I would rather explain to Jeff or to Charley, if he should happen upon me first, than to the Pied Piper who had unwittingly led me into this embarrassing plight. So I would postpone my screaming and pounding until that worthy had had more than ample time to get far away.

I never wanted to see that worthy again. I didn't care what he had been doing in our basement. I didn't care if he had sneaked down here with his shovel to bury an unabridged biography of the murderer, the victim's missing clothes, his missing furniture, or—

Kaufman's missing furniture!

The police had failed to locate it. No one had seen it being moved out of the apartment or out of the house. The reason for that was obvious; the furniture must still be in the house. Not in any of the apartments— the police had searched them thoroughly—but in the logical place, the only possible place. The cellar. It *had* to be there!

And I would find it. Then, instead of creeping shamefacedly out of this subterranean vault like a naughty and mentally retarded child of six, I could march triumphantly back into the daylight, head high, to take my place among the world's foremost deductive minds.

I snuffed out my cigarette and counted my matches. Nine. I would have to be systematic, careful but quick, no lost motion.

Eight matches later I had covered all but one corner and had seen no signs of furniture, Kaufman's or anyone else's. Thanks to Charley's sense of order, I had not even found the usual odds and ends that litter most basements.

But there was something curious about this final corner. Partitioned off by boards, it formed a small, square room. Saving my last match, I groped along the two accessible walls, feeling for some sort of opening. There was none. At least, none that I could find. That aroused my suspicion. I had to get into this place.

I lit my last match. The board wall before which I was standing reached clear to the ceiling. I went around the corner and looked at the other side. That partition stopped short about two feet lower. Just before the match burned my fingers I spied an old orange crate.

I stretched out my hand, dragged the crate to me, and climbed upon it. Then, summoning all the old tomboy in me, I shinnied over the wall and found myself dangling by my hands, my feet swinging in space.

This, I thought as I hung there, could be an old well, a bottomless pit, a cleverly camouflaged entrance to the New York sewerage system. Or it might be the place where Charley kept an unrivaled collection of bored boa constrictors. At any rate, I would soon know. I let go.

I dropped all of six inches and the unexpected promptness of my landing nearly jarred my head off. I groped around the four walls, crisscrossing and re-crisscrossing the square area. There was something on the floor that scrunched under my feet like bits of broken glass but, aside from that, the room was completely empty.

At a loss, I relaxed in a corner to get my bearings. I was puzzling over the possibility of an egress without the aid of my orange crate when the roof above me seemed to explode and a circular shaft of broad daylight streamed into my cozy nook. A big, strange-looking metal snout followed the daylight into the hole. And almost at once a thunderous roar filled the air and a hideous black torrent sprayed nauseating dust.

The ebony wave sluiced toward me, driving me farther back into my corner. My feet were buried in it and it was crawling up my legs before I realized what it was. Coal. Pea coal. The stuff I had ground under my feet was the remains of it. The gent with the shovel was the coal man. My secret room was the coal bin.

Although I knew I had too much competition, I opened my mouth to scream. I nearly strangled on the dust. My eyes and nose and mouth were filled with it. The tide had risen to my knees. I pulled one leg out, lost my balance, and sat down. A fresh splurge of anthracite, or possibly bituminous, poured into my lap. No, it wasn't bituminous, either. That was soft coal. This foul stuff hurt.

In my awkward position, one leg bent at the knee, the other stuck straight out like a Russian dancer, and both of them buried, I was unable to move from the waist down. Desperately I tried to bail the coal off with my hands, but it moved relentlessly up toward my shoulders.

My head was far below the top board of the wall. I knew now the reason for the pounding I had heard. My friend had put the removable boards on the side of the bin. That meant he expected his new load to reach the top. Far above my head. I was being buried alive!

This couldn't happen to me! I had a future. I was the girl my class had voted most likely to succeed. Not most likely to be caught in a coal bin. I was going to be one of America's leading actresses—It was creeping up over my shoulders now.

I wasn't ready to be buried alive. There were things I had to do. That button on Jeff's blue coat—that book overdue at the library, a five-cents-a-day book, too. I had an appointment at the dentist's—They mustn't find me with my teeth needing cleaning—It was crawling up my neck.

It wasn't fair; there were things that I wanted to do that I hadn't done. I'd never seen Niagara Falls, New York from the top of the Empire State, Jeff in tails and top hat, the dawn come up like thunder out of China cross the bay, Danny Kaye, Jeff on roller skates, Grant's Tomb. But I wouldn't think any more. I was getting morbid. It was touching my chin.

I took a deep breath. If this was to be my last I wanted it to be good. But the dust spoiled it for me; I choked and spluttered. I fought for air and finally, to my surprise, got some. The roar of the coal on the chute subsided, the coal itself dribbled to a stop. I was alive. And pleased.

"Hand me that shovel," a voice above me said. "I'll push it around."

The chute was withdrawn and a pair of feet took its place. My friend lowered himself and his shovel down into the bin.

"Hey!" I said.

His back was toward me and through the settling dust I could see it freeze. "Hey!" I said again. Without even looking around, he started back through the hole.

"Wait!" I shouted, "get me out of here!"

He stopped and slowly turned. His eyes moved searchingly all around my head until they finally focused on my face. He blinked; he gaped; his mouth dropped open.

I smiled at him reassuringly. "I'm Haila Troy," I said. "I live here."

"A helluva place to live!" he managed to gasp. "What—what the— why—hey! What are you doing here?"

"In a few minutes I'm leaving for Newcastle and I just wanted some coals—Will you please get me out of here?"

"Hey, Jim!"

I shut my eyes tight so that the expression on Jim's face might be lost to me. I couldn't have stood it.

Between the two of them, and the shovel, they finally got me mined and to the surface. They boosted me up through the hole. I didn't wait to thank them. I turned and fled into the house.

The full-length mirror in the bathroom reflected an even worse mess than I had expected. I was a shambles, a black shambles. My shoes, my stockings, my skirt and blouse, my face and neck and arms. My hair, which I liked to think of as raven, looked pale in comparison with the rest of me.

I heard a noise and turned to see Jeff standing in the doorway, examining me. He took a snowy-white handkerchief from his breast pocket and extended it in my direction.

"Haila," he said, "your mascara's running."

CHAPTER SEVEN

MY COURAGE FAILED ME at the tub's edge. I couldn't do it. Loaded down with Turkish towels, soap, washcloths, and brushes, I tried to sneak through the living room and into the kitchen. But Jeff turned from staring out into the garden just in time to catch me.

"If you say a word, Troy—" I threatened.

"Haila, did I ever tell you what happened in the kitchen sink?"

"Don't you dare!"

"One night Joe was throwing a little party. Very small, in fact. And a despondent midget—"

I slammed the door in his face. Thirty-five minutes, a bar of soap, and a box of Bab-O later, I emerged from the kitchen and my ebon state, exhausted, but recognizable. At least recognizable enough for Jeff to remark that it was nice seeing me again.

"Give me a cigarette, dear," I said, "and tell me about you and Hankins. Did he use a rubber hose on you?"

"I think he would have liked to. But somebody had borrowed it to put out a fire."

"Darling, please! I want to know. Did you convince Hankins that you never knew Kaufman?"

Jeff shook his head. "He insists that I did, and I didn't argue with him. I just sat there staring at his dirty shirt until he got embarrassed and threw me out."

"You're right about Hankins, the lug! Asking us to prove that this is our furniture!"

"Hmm. One thing worries me about him. I'm afraid he might be the type of cop that is wrong, but proves he's right."

"Jeff, this *is* our furniture and you *don't* know Kaufman!"

"How can I prove I never knew him? Get witnesses for every moment of my life? There's a much simpler way to remove Hankins from my neck, Haila."

"Tell me."

"Find out which one of the tenants knew Kaufman, had a motive to kill him, and did kill him."

"You think that's a *simpler* way?"

"Well, more interesting. We'll meet some people."

"Yes! Of which one out of seven is a murderer. That ratio is too low to suit me, Jeff. I'd rather be lonely or join the Greenwich Village Garden Club."

He sat down on a love seat. "Very well, dear. I'll wave to you from the gallows. Look up from your knitting and toss me a kiss. Two-handed, for old times' sake."

"Jeff! You don't really believe that Hankins suspects you! You want an excuse to try and solve this case. But if you start snooping around, it'll make you look more suspicious to Hankins. I have a feeling we shouldn't get mixed up in this."

"We are mixed up in it! It happened in our apartment, in our bathtub. Oh, I'm not worried about Hankins proving me the killer, but I bet at the moment I'm his number one suspect. And I bet he'll be spending more time on me for a long while to come than on anybody else. Don't you want to get him out of our hair and home as soon as possible?"

"Yes, but—"

"C'mon, get dressed and let's go about making discreet inquiries."

I groaned, but walked into the bedroom and started to slip out of my housecoat. I caught myself just in time. A scattering of Peeping Toms, who had put homicide on their sight-seeing itinerary, still lurked outside our naked bedroom windows. Making a mental note to wangle some kind of shades out of Charley or his boss, I scooped up my clothes and retreated to the middle room.

"Haila," Jeff called to me from the living room, "this isn't the first murder these four walls have seen."

"I'm beginning to hate these four walls," I wailed.

"Hankins told me about it. It was a long time ago, when the place was still a speakeasy. A local playboy was shot here by a gangster named Ziggy Koehler. The cops had been after Ziggy for years and this time they had him cold. Until a witness popped up at the last minute and gave Ziggy an airtight alibi. That witness was our little landlord."

"Turner! Oh, that explains all the innuendo between Hankins and him this morning."

"Right."

"How did you happen not to be here at Joe's the night of that murder? Were you sick, dear?"

"That was before I found Joe's."

"Jeff, did Turner just rent this place to him?"

"Yes. Turner didn't have anything else to do with it. I don't even remember having ever seen him around. Aren't you ready yet?"

"Umhum," I said, joining Jeff in the living room. "But you aren't. Your face is dirty."

"I know," Jeff said. "I noticed the other day it was getting dirty. Let's start at the top with Polly Franklin and work down."

Most women would have sputtered a thousand apologies had they and their apartment been found at five o'clock in the afternoon in the condition we found Polly Franklin, her two rooms, and bath. In the bedroom, the covers had been ripped off a studio couch and thrown across a chair in front of an open window. Other chairs were draped high with dresses, hats, and accessories. The big headless and footless bed in the living room was covered with an India print and littered with newspapers and magazines. Odd dishes, dirty ashtrays and more clothes were everywhere.

Polly, still wearing the tweed skirt and sweat shirt, laughed as she waved us in. "I've been sleeping all afternoon," she explained, "that's why the place isn't in more of a mess. Try and find a place to sit down, I dare you to! How did you like my restaurant? I saw the two of you there last night."

Still chatting away, she scraped a clearing on the bed and curled up in it. I moved three empty glasses off a straight-backed chair and sat down. Jeff eased himself onto the edge of a table. Polly gave him a long sidewise glance, then cocked her head and frankly inspected him. She turned to me and smiled.

"Congratulations, Mrs. Troy," she said.

"Thank you!"

"What?" Jeff, the old pretender, asked. "Miss Franklin, are the Hellions a baseball or a football team? And did you steal that jersey from your little brother?"

"I didn't steal it, you so and so, and the name is Polly! This sweater was given to me. By my son."

"You have a son?" I asked in surprise.

"Sure! He's twelve now. I have him up at the Carleton Academy in New Hampshire." She burst into her hearty guffaw at the expression on my face. "Don't look like that, darling. I was married. And divorced."

"Oh," I said.

"Bobby made the winning touchdown in this jersey. Then he presented it to me. Quite a ceremony! He made a speech, then I made a speech."

"Does Bobby look like you?" I asked.

"No, thank God! And not like his father, either. He's sort of a combination of Gary Cooper and Cary Grant. The best features of each, you understand. He swims like Weissmuller, hits like Joe DiMaggio and—well, athletically, he's all-around like Jim Thorpe, if you go back that far."

"Polly," Jeff said in a voice that proved he had been only half listening, "being right next door to Mike Kaufman, you should have heard his stuff being moved out."

A quick twinge of displeasure crossed her face. "I thought maybe you'd come up here to forget about Kaufman and murder. And I was cooperating."

"Thanks but about the furniture—"

"No," she said impatiently, "I didn't hear a thing. When I sleep, you could move out my bed and I wouldn't notice. Darling, I've told Hankins every damn thing I know. Which is nothing. And now let's forget all about it, shall we?"

"Don't you want to see justice done?" Jeff asked with mock sanctimoniousness.

"Oh, yes, indeedy, darling! But I hardly knew the man. Even though he lived next door to me and used to eat pretty often at my place, we hardly said more than twenty words to each other in the past three years. Why should I get gray worrying about who killed him? Let Hankins get gray, that's his job. I've got enough to worry about. Carleton is an expensive school, and Bobby needs new shoes every other week."

Jeff slid off the table, holding up a stamped and addressed envelope. "Could I mail this for you, Polly? We'll be going out."

Polly smiled and started to nod. Then, suddenly, she was on her feet and across the room. She snatched the letter from Jeff's hand and crumpled it behind her back. When she saw Jeff's confusion, hers doubled his.

"I'm sorry, darling, I—"

"That's all right, I shouldn't have—"

"No, that damn murder has got me." Her laugh was brittle. "I just don't want that letter mailed. It's for my brother and he arrived in town yesterday. He's coming to the joint for dinner tonight, and I'll tell him everything that I've written." She laughed again. "Nobody sees the grammar I commit unless it's absolutely necessary. Hey, I've got to get dressed and go to work! I'm late! Get out of here, you two! Come again, though, come all the time!"

We walked past the open door of Mike Kaufman's empty apartment and down the stairs to the fourth floor, the Misses Griffith's floor. As Jeff raised his hand to knock, I involuntarily grabbed his wrist.

"What, Haila?"

"I—don't know." But I did know. I was being silly. Last night, after our experience in Polly's restaurant, my imagination had been on edge. And when I had seen Miss Lucy Griffith staring at us from her window I had tried to make something of it. Common sense told me now that at the distance of four flights and in the meager light of a none too close street lamp it was stupid of me to jump to conclusions about what I had seen—or thought I had seen—in that face. And having become acquainted with the face's sister, Miss Charlotte Griffith, furthered the proof that my imagination had been working overtime.

I said to Jeff, "Go ahead, knock."

The door swung open a second after he had rapped upon it, and Charlotte Griffith's bulk almost filled the opening. Her smile was a welcome mixed with faint surprise. I thought that she was going to invite us in, but instead she said, "Wait just a second, won't you, please?"

Leaving us, she tiptoed awkwardly toward a door at the far end of the strangely furnished living room. Gilt-framed family pictures sagged on every wall, beaded curtains veiled the archway into an adjoining room, settees and chairs heavy with plush and ball-and-claw motif and rugs thick with faded floral patterns crowded the place. But evidently the sisters Griffith were also mild devotees of the *moderne*. Slick chromium book ends, a tubular vase of spun aluminum, a nest of ash trays of thick Swedish glass stood out anachronistically in all that Victorian somberness.

Miss Charlotte closed the far door with a sickroom softness and started back toward us. She took a few steps, hesitated, turned back, and for a moment listened. Then, with amazing quickness, she came to the doorway where we stood.

"All this excitement," she said apologetically, "has been too much for my sister."

"I'm sorry," Jeff said. "I'd hoped that we might be able to visit her. Does she like to have company?"

"Oh, yes, indeed, when she's strong enough. But for the past week she's been very poorly. And then this terrible business—"

"I know," Jeff said sympathetically.

"And that Mr. Hankins! He insisted on talking to her! What she could possibly have told him that would have any bearing on the case—" She had stopped to listen again. "Please excuse me now. Lucy is calling."

The door was closed firmly and quietly in our faces, leaving Jeff and me staring at each other.

"Did you hear Lucy call?" Jeff asked me.

"No."

"Neither did I."

"But we weren't listening, Jeff."

"I was listening while Miss Charlotte was listening."

"Eavesdropper."

"Haila, do you think that was Lucy you saw at the window last night?"

"I can't be sure, of course, but—who else could it have been?"

Jeff didn't mention any names. He took me by the arm, turned me around, and said, "Let's go visit the Carstairses."

It was a pleasure to be greeted as Scott greeted us. He pushed us into chairs, shoved rye highballs and cigarettes into our hands, and seemed genuinely glad to see us.

"Anne's just taking a shower, she'll be right with us," he said. He lifted his glass. "Well, here's to less murder and more good old-fashioned mayhem."

Jeff sighed. "They don't have mayhem like they used to have."

"Not like when I was a boy," Scott agreed. "It's the radio. People get mad at the comedians instead of each other."

Anne spoke from the doorway. Her voice was tight with strain. "My husband isn't always like this, Haila. Only on days when bodies are found."

"Darling!" Scott said sharply. He crossed the room and put his arm around Anne's shoulders. "Anne, no body was found. There wasn't any murder. Just for a little while. What do you say, darling?"

"All right, Scott." She raised her head and brushed a kiss across his cheek. "We won't talk about it; we won't even think about it."

Anne picked up her drink. She sat on the edge of a chair, holding the glass in both hands and looking down at it. The rest of us looked at her. Scott cleared his throat several times, as if in a valiant effort to find some word that wasn't murder.

Then Anne said quietly, "We've got to talk about it, we might as well. I know if I don't I'll become a shrieking neurotic. Jeff—"

"Yes, Anne?"

"We've been warned against you."

"By whom?"

"Hankins."

"Yeah," Scott said and grinned. "If you come around asking questions, we're to ignore you. Are you going to ask us questions?"

"If you do," Anne said, "veil them. So we won't be breaking the law right out in the open by answering them."

"I doubt if we'd have any answers, Anne," Scott said.

"That won't bother Jeff at all," I told them. "Go ahead, darling. Veil them a question."

"What I'd like to do," Jeff said, "is to throw a party and get everyone in this house roaring drunk. So they would tell me about themselves."

"What do you want to know about them?" Anne asked.

"I'm afraid it'd be a hell of a dull party, Jeff," Scott said. "One struggling commercial artist—yours truly—and his enchanting wife. One mousy little landlord, one lady owner of a restaurant, one pair of middle-aged sisters, and Mr. Lingle. A nucleus for a Sunday school class if ever I saw one."

"What does Lingle do?"

"Nothing," Scott said. "He's retired."

"A retired art dealer," Anne added. "And that sounds intriguing to me."

"Yeah." Scott chuckled. "He spends all his time nowadays wandering nostalgically from museum to exhibit to gallery, looking at a mess of beautiful pictures. But don't mind me. I'm jealous. All illustrators are thwarted painters, and I'll never paint a good picture."

"You will, Scott," Anne said firmly. She turned to me. "Scott won't let me see any of the things that he's done at the League. He says they're foul but I know they're not. I'm sure they're wonderful."

"I'll say." Scott laughed.

"I can sympathize with you, Scott," I said. "Jeff thinks I'm a wonderful actress. Don't you, darling?"

"Umhum. I liked you best in that part where you kept running up and down those stairs. Your heels—they twinkled. Anne, how long has Lucy Griffith been an invalid?"

"She isn't exactly an invalid," Anne said.

"No? I got the impression that she was practically bedridden."

"She is," Scott said. "She's been sick as long as we've lived here."

"But not sick enough to be in bed," Anne said. "There are times when she's well enough to take walks. Why, I met her in the vestibule just yesterday or the day before."

"No, sweetheart, you're wrong. She's been lower than usual lately. I think she had some sort of an attack last week."

"But I did see her! At least in the last two or three days!" Anne's voice rose, giving the discussion much more importance than, I felt sure, it deserved.

"All right," Scott said, "you saw her yesterday."

"Don't humor me, Scott! I'm not a child."

"Anne," Scott said gently, "I know you're not a child. I'm not, either, but this damn murder has got me, too. Let's all have another drink, shall we?"

"If Lucy's an invalid," Anne hurried on, "how can her sister work five days a week at that employment agency? Nobody comes in to take care of Lucy while she's gone."

"Let's all have another drink, shall we, Anne?" Scott repeated deliberately.

"Yes, let's!" I said quickly.

Scott was measuring the rye when he spoke again. "The point is," he said, "that every single person in this house is so respectable that he or she could be a friend of Mother's."

"All but one," Anne said quietly. "Your mother wouldn't pal around with a murderer."

"And," Jeff added, "I doubt if Mike Kaufman numbered many mothers among his best friends."

"Mike Kaufman," Scott said. "There was a lone wolf to end lone wolves. How anyone could have got to know that guy well enough to want to murder him is—"

Anne jumped to her feet, both hands pressed hard against her temples. "Oh, let's not talk about it."

"It was you who wanted to, Anne."

"I know. But the day began with murder and—well, I can't stand it ending with the same thing! Let's discuss politics or dog-training or something! Please!"

Scott passed around the drinks quickly and we sat there making desultory conversation as we sipped. It wasn't any good. No matter what we talked about each of us knew what the others were thinking. Who killed Mike Kaufman? Which one of the people now under this very roof had murdered a man last night?

Jeff and I finally bowed out, accepting Anne's and Scott's ardent invitations to come again, immediately. As we continued our tour by descending to the next floor, I couldn't help remarking to Jeff that even a murder had its good points. It had made Anne forget how unenthusiastic she had been about our moving into 39 Gay Street.

Watching Jeff knock on Henry Lingle's door, I began to feel as if I were married to a Fuller brush man. And I didn't like it. I was grateful to Mr. Lingle for not being at home. But our landlord was in, very much so. His tiny feet were encased, slightly, in battered old bedroom slippers. The rest of him was lost in what might have been his first bathrobe. Seeing that he was in no mood for guests, I quickly put our call on a business basis by asking him for window shades.

"I've ordered them—new ones, Mrs. Troy, but there's such a rush on October first. If you'd moved in when you planned now—" His voice trailed off, leaving the track of a gentle reproof behind it.

"Isn't there something you could let us have temporarily?"

Mr. Turner wrinkled his brow in thought, then a pale, hopeful smile cracked his face. "I have a screen that would cover one of your windows but—well, I'll show it to you."

We followed him into his little drearily furnished apartment. In one corner a kitchenette was camouflaged by a dull-brown monk's-cloth curtain which evidently even Mr. Turner had found depressing. For in front of it stood the screen.

For years George Turner must have assiduously been clipping newspapers, the most pictorial magazines and the Police Gazette. Then, feeling at last that he had a comprehensive anthology of feminine dishabille, he had artistically mounted it on the screen and covered it with a coat of shellac, so that neither rain nor sleet nor hail could deny it to posterity.

Before I had a chance to shout a firm no-thank-you, Jeff had folded the work of lurid art under his arm.

"Just the thing, Mr. Turner," he was saying. "I'll give up to a thousand dollars for it."

Our landlord flushed in quick embarrassment, and Jeff's next remark did nothing toward helping him regain his poise. "I understand," he said chattily, "that you're an old friend of Ziggy Koehler's."

Turner swallowed and said hastily, almost frantically, "That was a long time ago, Mr. Troy. All over now, all forgotten."

"That murder and this one are just a coincidence, huh?"

"Yes, that's it. Just a coincidence, Mr. Troy. Ziggy Koehler is dead now, he was killed in an auto accident. There isn't any connection between Mr. Kaufman being murdered and—and the other one, none at all. And Mr. Troy," his voice dropped to a pleading whisper, "I wish you'd forget about—Ziggy Koehler. If the other tenants knew—well, it wouldn't be good for the house."

"None of the present tenants were living here then?"

"Oh, no, all new tenants since that time. That was so long ago. It's all over."

"Well, thanks for the screen, Mr. Turner," Jeff said. "It's lovely."

Back in our own apartment, Jeff leaned our new *objet d'art* against the wall without, surprisingly, even glancing at a one of the shameless hussies who overpopulated it.

"Scott's right," he thought aloud. "A group of less suspicious looking suspects I have never seen. If this were a cookie-snitching job instead of a murder, I could believe one of them did it. Haila, speaking of cookies, I'm hungry. Let's go to Polly's."

"It's too early for dinner," I objected.

"Not, I gather, for Polly's brother. I want to see him."

"Polly's brother! Jeff, you can't make a suspect out of him. He doesn't even live in New York, let alone in this house."

"He was in New York yesterday, wasn't he? And he's connected to this house through Polly."

"Darling, this murder has you so stymied that you're clutching at you-know-whats! Frankly, straws! Polly's brother, indeed!"

"All right, I'll go alone. You can stay here alone, Haila. Take a bath."

CHAPTER EIGHT

ON THE WAY TO POLLY'S RESTAURANT I had to gallop to keep abreast of my husband, who had suddenly turned into a ball of liquid fire. Crossing Sheridan Square I saved his life three times.

I realized then that until this murder had been put on ice, I would have to do his seeing, hearing, and thinking in all matters not homicidal. Otherwise he would certainly perish by traffic, nicotine poisoning, brain strain, lack of sleep, or hunger. I was glad that one of the suspects in our little murder manse owned a restaurant. That might help me avert at least one of my husband's perils.

We spotted Polly immediately as she sat at a corner table opposite a thin and angular young man. Unless we had known, we would never have suspected any relationship between the two. His hair was as dark as hers was blond, his face as sharp and pointed as hers was round.

Polly saw us threading our way between the already crowded tables and a flicker of annoyance twisted her mouth. Then, instantly, it was chased away by her habitual sunny beam. She stood up and waved.

"Well, the Troys again! My place is habit-forming, isn't it? I hope. This is my baby brother. Jeff and Haila Troy, neighbors of mine."

The baby brother rose to his full six feet and stood towering over his baby sister as he mumbled something pleasant and unintelligible.

"How are you, Mr. Bruhl?" Jeff asked. "We heard that you—"

He stopped; he couldn't very well go on. The questioning frown that creased the young man's face, the stony setness that crept over his sister's, challenged any continuation. We stood in a confused and awkward silence that Polly at last dissolved.

"My brother's name," she said, "is Ward Franklin. Franklin was my maiden name."

"I'm sorry," Jeff said, and laughed. "I don't know where I picked up that other name."

Ward Franklin said heartily, "Sit down, won't you? I want to hear all the gory details of this murder. Polly's been holding out on me; she says I'm too young. Sit down, Mrs. Troy."

"But we'll crowd you, won't we?" I said, eyeing the tiny table.

Polly pushed me firmly down in her chair and pulled another from a nearby table for Jeff. "I've got to go bully the help," she told us, "so please sit here. It's the best table in the house, the only one that doesn't wobble. And, Ward, be nice to Jeff. I hear that he's a very clever detective."

"Diabolically clever, please," Jeff called after her.

Polly disappeared into the kitchen; we ordered dinner and Ward another Scotch and soda. For the next half hour we chatted about the murder, the restaurant, Ward's business. He was on a selling trip, he told us, and would be in New York only another day or two.

"I'd like to get up to New Hampshire and see Bobby," he said. "I usually manage to squeeze in a visit with him whenever I'm in the East. But this time I'll have to be back in Chicago by Friday."

"Bobby sounds like a great kid," Jeff said.

Uncle Ward beamed proudly and with no more ado was off on what seemed to be the entire Franklin family's favorite topic. It was all Jeff could do to slip a word in edgewise. And, in fact, his usual amount was reduced to a mere one cent's worth. "Bobby's father?" he asked. "When does he get to see him?"

Ward Franklin's mouth stretched in a thin smile. "Never," he said. "Polly was awarded full custody of Bobby at the divorce. His father's never seen him since then."

"But doesn't he—doesn't he want to?" I asked.

The smile stretched even farther. It became almost malicious. "He'd like to see him, all right. He'd like to have him. And there isn't anything on God's green earth he wouldn't do to get him. Or hasn't done, for that matter. First he tried to starve my sister into giving the child to him. But Polly fixed that. She opened a restaurant and made a go of it. And how! Look at this place! She's got a gold mine here."

"So that," Jeff said, "was the end of the father."

The spiteful look was back again in the young man's face, making it appear older. "No. That was the beginning. Next on his list was to prove that Polly was an unfit mother. He bribed her employees, he hired detectives, he even spied on her himself—and he's still at it. One swell guy my sister married!" A shrug, partly amused, partly sardonic, followed Franklin's frown. "Oh, well, let him waste his money and his time. He doesn't have a chance in hell. Just seeing Polly with Bobby for a minute would prove to anyone he's the luckiest kid in the world to have her for a mother."

I didn't see Polly come back. I thought she was still in the kitchen until I heard her voice behind me. She was standing right in back of my chair and her eyes, all the friendly warmth in them gone, were on her brother. Her voice was cold as she said, "You're wanted on the phone, Ward. You can use the one in the kitchen. I'll show you."

Jeff watched them until they were out of sight, then he turned back to his apple pie, jabbing it thoughtfully with his fork.

"You know, Haila," he said, "when I called Ward Franklin Mr. Bruhl—"

"That was brilliant of you, darling."

"It turned out to be. His name isn't Bruhl."

"Certainly not. It's Franklin. Where did you pick up Bruhl, anyway? Out of a crossword puzzle?"

"Uh-uh. It was the name on the letter Polly said she'd written to her brother. I wonder why she thought a letter addressed to one Jacob Bruhl who lives at 507 West Twelfth Street, New York City, would ever be delivered to one Ward Franklin who lives in Chicago."

"Oh, Jeff, stop straining! It was probably a typographical error on Polly's part. There's nothing at all suspicious about her or her brother—"

Before I had finished speaking, Jeff had beckoned a waiter to the table. "I want to make a phone call," he told the man.

The waiter pointed to the two booths at the far end of the room, the ones in which Mike Kaufman had made, and I had listened to, his fatal call.

"I get claustrophobia in booths," Jeff said. "Can't I use the one in the kitchen?"

"There's no phone in the kitchen," the waiter said. "Those booths are the only phones in the place."

"Thanks," Jeff said "Will you bring us a check?"

"No check. Miss Franklin's orders."

"There!" I gloated, as the man moved to another table. "See what a nice person Polly is?"

"She's nice to us," Jeff agreed. "But that doesn't mean she was always nice to—oh, say, Mike Kaufman, for instance. What was her brother saying to us that made her call him off with that phone gag? What is it about Jacob Bruhl that spoils her sunny disposition? A sunny disposition like that shouldn't be spoiled. It's up to us, as good citizens, to point that out to Mr. Bruhl. And immediately."

We stood for a few minutes on Twelfth Street looking at the narrow, three-story building. The clapboard front was peeling its ancient gray paint. Its windows were dirty and heavily shaded. In fact, only the two enormous warehouses between which it was wedged kept number 507 from tumbling right out into the street.

"I'd say," Jeff remarked, "that Mr. Jacob Bruhl runs an inn for traveling ghouls. Would you like to wait out here, Haila?"

"I'd love to, but I won't. Lead on."

There were no name plates outside the warped and sagging doorway, and no answer to the bell. Jeff rattled the knob, and the door creaked open. We stood in a dismal vestibule whose only furnishings consisted of a three-legged table littered with advertisements and laundry lists. A cracked and smeary mirror hung above it. Almost immediately a door at the other end of the hall opened and a huge, untidy woman waddled toward us.

"Something you want?" she asked in a nasal voice.

Jeff bowed from the ankles. "We're calling on a friend of ours who lives here. Mr. Jacob Bruhl. Is he at home?"

In the dreary light of the one naked bulb overhead, we could see the angry frown that spread across her face. She planted her hands on the roll of her hips in a gesture of belligerence.

"I'm sick of this," she shouted. "It ain't funny any more. If it's a joke, then I don't like it."

Jeff said quickly, "It's not a joke. I wanted to see Mr. Bruhl. He lives here, doesn't he?"

"He does not! And I'll thank people to stop running in here and pestering me about him."

"Have there been many people inquiring about Mr. Bruhl?"

"Too many! Off and on for a year or more. And I got enough to do without being bothered with them."

"Do you remember what any of them looked like? Could you describe—"

"No, I could not! I didn't care what they looked like. I told them no Bruhl lived here and that took more time than I had to waste."

"Perhaps," Jeff suggested. "Mr. Bruhl did live here once and moved—"

She interrupted him sharply. "Don't you try to tell me who lived here and who didn't! I been running this boardinghouse myself for twenty years. I guess I ought to know who lived in it. No Jake Bruhl lives here now or ever did! And good night to you!"

On our way back to Gay Street Jeff spoke once. "Bruhl has to live there," he muttered. "Why would Polly Franklin be so frantic about a letter to a man whose correct address she doesn't even have?"

"Huh?" I asked. "Repeat that, please."

But Jeff had already wrapped himself in one of his mental straitjackets and there he stayed until we were back at number thirty-nine. In the small outside vestibule, a tall, slender man was fumbling in the depths of a mailbox. I saw Jeff squint at the black-and-white name plate above the open box and he snapped out of his trance. Henry Lingle, the one suspect that Jeff had been unable to lay his hands upon, had practically fallen in his lap.

It came as no great surprise to me that in the next minute or two Jeff had introduced himself to our upstairs neighbor and invited him to our house for a drink.

With only a slight murmuring about the lateness of the hour, Henry Lingle accepted. He dutifully admired the bedroom into which we stepped, but his eyes lighted with real amusement when they happened to land on Mr. Turner's screen. Smiling, he moved toward the window to inspect it.

"George Turner," he told us whimsically, "has made a great sacrifice for you. I know how dear that art collection is to him. You should feel extremely grateful."

Assuring him that we did, we led him through the apartment and into the living room. There Jeff deposited him in a chair and soon had drinks for the three of us.

I slipped off my shoes surreptitiously, curled my feet up under me, and tried hard to concentrate on the conversation that was filling the room. Henry Lingle had begun to talk in his breezy, amiable fashion; theater for my sake, photography for Jeff's, and finally painting and painters. I knew that he was trying to take his own mind, as well as ours, off the gruesome events of the day. But in spite of his efforts I couldn't forget that tonight I would be sleeping under the same roof with a murderer—a careful, brutal murderer who had drowned one of his neighbors and left no trail behind.

Then Jeff made me ashamed of myself. He was undertaking the full responsibility of our guest and treading where he should have feared to tread, among the Old Masters.

"Give me Holbein," Jeff was saying, as one might say give me Joe Louis. "I'm a Holbein man. I go through the Metropolitan Museum and when I come away the only picture I can remember is Holbein's portrait of Sir Thomas More. He made More look like the kind of a guy I could pal around with on a Saturday night."

Lingle laughed. "You're right. That picture is one of my favorites, too. I've spent, all told, a good many hours up at the Metropolitan looking at Sir Thomas."

"Aw," Jeff said, "they don't come any better than Tom."

"Or Holbein, for that matter." Lingle smiled.

Jeff named the other Old Masters he remembered, made pithy and inaccurate remarks about each, then got to the subject he had been heading toward ever since he had pounced upon the art dealer in the hallway, the murder of Mike Kaufman.

"Mr. Lingle," he said, "did you hear anything last night that might have been the furniture being moved out of the house?"

Lingle shook his head. "You know, I'm inclined to think that furniture is a myth. Or perhaps someone did see or hear it leave the house and is afraid to admit it for fear of becoming involved in the murder."

"That could be," Jeff conceded.

"And the police seem so positive that someone in this house is the murderer. That could have frightened any one of the tenants into silence."

"It's pretty hard to believe," I said, "that one of the people I've met here could have—could be a murderer."

Lingle nodded understandingly. "Yes, I know. That thought's been following me all day. That one—well, actually, one of *us* who live in this house, one of the people I've been seeing almost every day for such a long time could possibly be guilty of such a crime." He snuffed out his cigarette and rose abruptly. "It was kind of you to invite me in. But it's time we should all be in bed, I suppose. We've had a strenuous day. Good night, Mrs. Troy. Mr. Troy."

Jeff waited until we heard Lingle's door slam on the floor above us, then he said, "That guy's a phony!"

I gaped at him. "A phony what?"

"Retired art dealer, for instance."

"You, with your knowledge of art," I jeered, "can tell that!"

"I happen to know about Holbein's Sir Thomas More. I helped the boss take a picture of it for a magazine layout of Holbein. And we didn't take the picture at the Metropolitan. Holbein's Sir Thomas More is in the Frick Collection."

"Jeff, you deliberately tricked Mr. Lingle, you louse!"

"A retired art dealer ought to know where one of his favorite pictures is hung. Especially if he's spent hours looking at it."

"It might have been a slip of his tongue."

"It wasn't his tongue; it was mine. I said it was in the Metropolitan and he didn't correct me."

"Maybe he was being polite, dear."

"People aren't polite about their own fields, they're educational. I can see you not correcting somebody who said Lynn Fontanne was married to Mickey Rooney!"

"All right, go ahead and suspect everyone on earth for the murder of Mike Kaufman. Suspect Mike Kaufman and see if I care. I'm going to bed. And besides, why would anyone pretend he was a retired art dealer?"

"If you're hiding, you have to have something to hide behind. That's common knowledge, a simple physical fact."

"Oh, be quiet! I wish this were Saturday night so you and Sir Thomas More could pal around together."

CHAPTER NINE

I LEFT JEFF IN THE LIVING ROOM and started off for bed. It had been only about thirteen hours since the discovery of the corpse in our garden, but already my brain and body felt centenarian.

Summer was still lingering in New York as if it couldn't make up its mind whether to go to Florida or California for the winter. I lowered both bedroom windows from the top, the stout iron bars stretching their length making that a safe move, and placed Mr. Turner's screenful of buxom beauties in front of the one nearest the bed. It was the door that was the problem. Tomorrow, I vowed, I would either get a lock from Mr. Turner or I would start picketing the place. I was about to return to the living room to ask Jeff how one locked a lockless door when I heard the knock. It was a soft, almost timid rapping, but there was an urgency in it, too.

Anne Carstairs was standing in the hallway outside, one hand clutching the collar of her quilted bathrobe tight around her neck, the other upraised to knock again. The soft, fleece-lined slippers she wore dropped her height a good two inches, and with her curly hair tied up in a bright-red ribbon, she looked like a little girl. A frightened little girl, just escaped from some lurid nightmare.

"Haila, may I—could I come in for a little while?"

"Anne, of course!"

I took her hand and drew her inside, then closed the door. When I turned she was sitting on the edge of the bed, watching me. The light from the lamp fell on her face. It was dead white. Her eyes were dark

80

and wide, the pupils dilated, and her hand, still clutching the collar of her
robe, was clenched so tightly that the knuckles were chalk-colored.

I went over quickly and sat beside her. "Anne, what is it? What's
happened to you?"

For a second she didn't answer, then she burst out angrily, "Probably
nothing, Haila! I'm nervous—being up there all alone—and I guess
I've just got a fine case of willies."

"I don't blame you, Anne," I said. "This has been dreadful for you.
You seeing the—that thing in the garden first and having to report it. It
must've been awful."

"It was. I guess I deserve to have the willies tonight, don't I?" She
smiled, but only one corner of her mouth turned up. "And when you
have the willies you imagine things, don't you?"

"Yes, Anne, you do."

"No!" She threw her head back and went on harshly. "Haila, I didn't
imagine this! I did hear it!"

"Hear what?"

"The knock on the door."

"Start at the beginning, Anne, tell me."

She took a deep breath in an effort to steady her voice. "I was
reading in bed, just a little while ago. There was a knock on the door,
and I called and asked who it was. There wasn't any answer. I crept
into the living room and listened. I couldn't hear any footsteps going
away or anything at all. Finally, I got together enough courage and
opened the door. There was no one there, no one."

"But Anne, you must've—It would be easy to be mistaken about a
knock—"

She interrupted me defiantly. "Somebody knocked on our door and
when he heard my voice, he sneaked away. I know it, Haila! And that
isn't all. They're watching me—all of them, every minute they're watching me."

"Who, Anne?"

"The people in this house. When I came down here just now, I met
Polly Franklin on the stairs. She went up to her place, but she didn't go
in. She stood there on the landing, watching me. I could feel her eyes all
the way down here. And Miss Griffith—the old one, came out of her
apartment and asked me where I was going. And when I got to the
second floor, Mr. Lingle's door was just closing. He'd been watching

me, too. I don't know why they're doing it; I don't know what it's all about. But I'm frightened, Haila, terribly frightened."

I tried to sound calm and reassuring. "Anne, they're not watching you, not really. They're all nervous and upset themselves, just as you are. When they hear someone on the stairs, they have to know who it is, what that person is doing. Can't you understand that?"

"Yes," Anne said slowly, "perhaps I do understand it, but it doesn't help. It doesn't make me want to stay up there alone."

She was still sitting on our bed, her shoulders hunched, her head bowed, terrified and miserable. The sight of Anne like that made me angry.

"Why in heaven's name," I demanded, "didn't Scott stay at home tonight? He shouldn't have left you all alone when you're feeling this way!"

She said quickly, "He doesn't know, Haila. And I couldn't tell him. I couldn't have him know."

"Why!"

"Well, then he *would* have stayed home. He would have missed his class at the League—"

"Anne!" It was all I could do to keep from shaking her. "Do you mean that Scott Carstairs wouldn't rather miss a class or two at the League than to have you driven into nervous prostration? When he finds out about this I bet he'll turn you over his knee and—"

"He won't find out," she said. Her mouth had settled in a thin, stubborn line. "I won't tell him."

"You won't have to, darling. I'm going to butt in at this point. I'm going to borrow your telephone and call the League right now."

She was across the room, standing flat against the door. "You're not going to call him," she said between her teeth. "I'm not going to let you."

I tried to push her aside. "Anne, don't be childish. This self-sacrifice is stupid. I'm going to tell Scott what's happening down here."

Her face flushed an angry red, and her eyes shot sparks at me. Then, just as suddenly, all her fury vanished, and she crumpled against the door.

"It's no use calling him, Haila," she said at last. The words were little more than a whisper. "Scott—Scott won't come."

I looked at her in amazement. "What do you mean? Of course he'll come. When he knows—"

"He does know." She walked wearily across the room to the window and stood looking out on Gay Street. "I've been lying to you, Haila. Scott does know how frightened I am. I told him. I begged him to stay with me tonight—or take me with him. He wouldn't."

For a moment I couldn't speak. Anne's husband had refused to— but I didn't believe it. The Scott Carstairs I had met that afternoon was not the same young man that Anne was talking about now. But Anne was telling the truth. The flat hopelessness of her words made that terribly evident.

"Darling," I said, going to her, "what is it? What's the matter?"

With her back still turned to me she shook her head. The little red bow on it bobbed merrily, mocking her unhappiness. "I don't know, Haila. Everything, I guess. Our marriage hasn't turned out to be the beautiful thing we dreamed up. It's no go, Haila, it's a bust."

"That isn't true, it can't be. You mustn't let this murder make you imagine things."

"No. It isn't the murder. It started to happen a long time ago, almost right after we were married. Scott changed; he changed all of a sudden. He isn't happy any more. Not with me, at any rate. I don't seem to matter now. There's only one thing that does. Money. Making money, lots of it. He slaves all day at the agency, he studies every night at the League, weekends he works on his illustrations at a studio someplace uptown."

"But if he wants to be a good painter, Anne—"

She shook her head sadly. "No, it isn't that. If he were doing this to be a good painter, you know I'd do anything, go through anything to help him. But it's only the money he wants! We scrimp and we save for no reason at all! We never spend anything, not even time with each other." She pushed her hair back and ran nervous fingers through it. "Maybe if we could strand ourselves on an island where wampum is the only legal tender, we might have a chance. But this way—" Her voice trailed off dismally.

"Anne," I said softly, "is that why, when we moved in—"

"Yes. I hated it when you came here to live. I didn't want to see you, to have you find out. Oh, Haila, can't you see? I've failed so badly in everything I've ever tried; all my life I've failed. I wrecked any career

I might have had by my stupidity. And now I've wrecked my marriage by—I—I don't know what I did, even!"

"Oh, Anne."

She wheeled around. "Don't pity me!" she said fiercely. Then she came to me and took my hand. "Haila, I'm sorry. Please forget all I've said. I'm so tired and—Couldn't I stay here tonight? I'm afraid to go back up there alone."

"Of course! I'll fix up the studio couch, Anne. You crawl into our bed until I get yours ready."

I went into the living room and explained briefly to Jeff what had happened. He helped me make up the studio couch. Anne was almost asleep when I went back to get her. With her eyes half closed she smiled at me, crawled into her bed, and mumbled good night.

I went back to my room, crawled under the covers, and closed my eyes. I didn't want to talk, not even to Jeff. My mind was full of Anne and her story. It couldn't be true. The murder, I told myself, and the resulting excitement had been too much for her.

Jeff came in and sat on the edge of the bed and put his arms around me. "Don't worry about them, Haila," he whispered.

"But Anne loves him, Jeff."

"I know, but—tomorrow, Haila. Good night."

"Good night. Jeff?"

"Yeah?"

"I'm glad there's no chance of you ever making any money."

"Why would I ever want to make any money?"

"That's what I mean. Good night, Jeff."

I burrowed deeper under the covers and closed my eyes again. But ten minutes later the light by the bedside was still shining brightly and keeping me awake. I rolled over to protest and found Jeff sitting on the edge of the bed, his elbows on his knees, his chin in his hands. He was minutely examining our landlord's collection of luscious lovelies. I was darned if I would be a party to that; I reached up and snapped off the light.

"Haila, don't!"

"You can leer at those babes in the cold light of day."

"Turn it on!"

I turned it on quickly. Jeff leaned over, dragged me across the bed to his side, and pointed. In the margin of a picture of a girl in a fragmentary bathing-suit, I saw faint scribbling. I bent closer.

"Jeff! It says, 'J. Bruhl'! Could that be—"

"Who else? It also says 507 West Twelfth Street." Jeff got up and strode around the room. "Haila, George Turner has a connection with this Bruhl. And so has Polly Franklin. I've got a hunch that in some way Mr. J. Bruhl is tied up with this whole business here."

"Jeff, it doesn't seem possible that little Mr. Turner—he couldn't have—"

"Your little Mr. Turner once alibied a very illegitimate and dangerous character out of going to his just reward. Don't forget that. But why in hell are both he and Polly Franklin having to-do with a man named Jake Bruhl at 507 West Twelfth Street? Especially since no one by that name ever lived there?"

"Maybe that landlady was lying and he does live there."

"Well, whether he does or not, people write letters to him there. And something happens to those letters. I'm going to find out what."

"How?"

"Write to Jacob Bruhl myself. Haila, take a letter."

"Take it yourself, please, darling. I'm too tired."

Jeff stuffed a blank piece of paper in an envelope, scratched the address on it, and dashed away to the corner to mail it. He was back before I could get to sleep. Through half-closed eyes I watched him get ready for bed, readjust the screen before the window, then turn out the lamp.

I don't know how much later it was that I awoke. At first I thought it was morning, for the room was filled with light. Then I realized that the arc light on Gay Street was tossing its glare through our one unscreened window, filling the room with it. I rolled over on my other side.

That didn't do any good. It was still as bright as day. I could clearly see my dressing-table against the far wall, the figures on its cretonne skirt, the glasses and bottles and jars on its mirrored top. I could see the dresser along the wall in back and, beside me, the hall door. And I could see something else, too. I shook the sleep out of my eyes and looked again.

Even then I thought it must be a trick of lighting. There had been no noise, no rattling or clicking. There had been no footsteps in the hall. But, even as I looked now, the doorknob turned. Slowly and deliberately it was revolving. Then it stopped. The door began to move almost imperceptibly open. First the crack was hairline, then it widened to an inch. It held there.

Without moving my eyes, I stretched my right hand back and shook Jeff by the shoulder. I could feel him sit bolt upright.

"Haila, what is it?" he whispered, wide awake.

I pointed to the door.

It moved slowly, silently back into its frame. The knob, in reverse, turned and then stopped. There was still no sound.

Jeff slipped out of bed and tiptoed quickly to the door. He listened a moment, his ear glued to the paneling. Then, abruptly, he flung it open and stepped into the hall.

I crept out after him. Even in the dim yellow hall light we could see that the place was completely empty. We looked up the staircase. There was no one, nothing to be seen. The lights on each landing were burning. Jeff tried the street entrance. It was locked from the inside. The entire house was smothered in absolute silence.

Jeff led me back into the bedroom. He shut the door and put a straight-backed chair under the knob, bracing it firmly. Then he sat down beside me on the bed. He softly whistled, off-key, *Silent Night, Holy Night*—

"Jeff," I asked, "did you see what I saw?"

He contemplated me for a moment, then shook his head. "You were dreaming, Haila."

"Jeff, don't! I'm not a child!"

"All right, sweetheart, since you asked for it. Somebody was trying to get in here."

"So Anne was right, after all," I said slowly. "Somebody is after her."

"But nobody knows that she's here, do they?"

"Everybody knows it! Everybody in the house. They watched her come down here and—Jeff, don't tell her about this."

"You don't have to tell me," Anne's voice said from the doorway. "I know what happened."

Her eyes were fastened on the chair braced under the doorknob. She was staring at it in fascinated horror.

"Anne," Jeff said, starting toward her. Then he stopped.

In the silence we heard what he had heard. The fumbling at the street door, the sound of its opening, the light footsteps in the hall. Jeff slid the chair away and flung open the door.

Scott Carstairs was already halfway up the first flight and he turned in surprise. "Hello, Jeff!" he said and came down the stairs. At our doorway, he stopped, his eyes on his wife.

"Anne! What is it? What's the matter?"

"Nothing."

Scott looked from her to Jeff to me. "Something's wrong!"

I said, "Anne was nervous, Scott. Frightened. She came to stay with us."

"Oh, that!" Scott grinned deprecatingly, then crossed to Anne and put his arm around her. "I don't blame Anne's imagination for playing tricks on her after what happened in your garden."

She pulled away from him and took two quick steps toward me. "Tell him, Haila. He—he may believe you."

"Someone knocked on your door tonight, Scott, then when they discovered that Anne was still awake they vanished. And just now, only a few minutes ago, someone tried to get in here. Everybody in the house knew that Anne was with us, too; they had watched her come down. Somebody's trying to—to get her, Scott."

Scott stared incredulously at me, then he turned to Jeff for some denial of my statement. Jeff said, "Haila's right."

Scott stood silent, looking at the three of us for a moment. Then his lips tightened in a thin line. "I don't care," he said harshly, "what you saw, or thought you saw. Anne's in no danger. Do you think I'd have left her alone if she were?" He turned to her, making no attempt to conceal his impatience. "You're being silly and hysterical, darling."

"I'm not! Oh, Scott, hasn't what Jeff and Haila told you proved that I'm not? Something's going on in this house, I tell you, something strange and terrible. And I'm—I'm in the center of it, somehow. They're all watching me! As if they were afraid that something was going to happen to me—"

"Anne!" Scott's face was suddenly suffused with irritation. His hands reached out to Anne as if they were going to shake her. Then, with a great effort he controlled himself. "Anne, this is scared-kid stuff. It isn't like you." His voice dropped to a gentleness. "Anne, come on, let's go home, darling, shall we?"

Anne didn't look at him when she spoke. Her voice was cold and expressionless. "All right, Scott. Thanks for everything, Haila. And forgive me for—for bothering you with my hysterics."

We watched her climb the stairs, like a wooden soldier, and Scott, his face angry again, following her.

I looked at Jeff. There must be something that we could do. But he shook his head. And the expression on his face made me ask, "What is it, Jeff? What's—"

"It's Scott Carstairs. I wonder what he knows that makes him so positive that Anne is in no danger? So damned sure that the murderer isn't going to harm her?"

CHAPTER TEN

IT WAS COLD and a gray drizzling rain was falling when, at eight o'clock the next morning, we stationed ourselves at the entrance of the warehouse to the right of number 507. We had arrived none too early, for almost immediately the blue-coated figure of a postman swung around the corner and started up Twelfth Street.

He was only a few steps from the dilapidated boardinghouse when Jeff flipped away his cigarette and, sauntering along with overdone casualness, followed him into the house. Then the mailman reappeared and, a moment later, Jeff came slowly down the steps. His face, as he walked back to me, was wrinkled in deep perplexity.

"Well?" I demanded. "Who took the letter?"

"Nobody."

"Nobody? You mean—What do you mean?"

"It wasn't delivered."

"It didn't make the first mail, then," I said. "After all, you didn't post it until late last night."

"By dog sled—Pekingese," Jeff said positively, "it should have arrived in the first delivery. But I'll hang around and catch the next one, anyway. Haila, why don't you go home and wait for me there?"

"All right. I'll see about a lock for our door. Jeff, are you going to work today?"

"I doubt it. I'll call the studio and explain."

"So long, Jeff."

"Good-by, Haila. Give my regards to your family."

As I walked back to Gay Street, I had to buck the tide of the nine-o'clock shift that poured toward the subways. Smart young girls trying to simultaneously light their after-breakfast cigarettes, read their morning mail, and look over their makeups. Smart young men trying to simultaneously light their after-breakfast cigarettes, read their morning mail, and look over the smart young girls. On Sheridan Square I ran into Ward Franklin. He paused only long enough to bid me a cheery good morning, then hurried on.

Charley was lackadaisically going through the motions of polishing the brass on the front door of number thirty-nine, and I pounced on him at once.

"Charley," I said sternly, "what about a lock for our door?"

"I don't know anything about it. Listen, Mrs. Troy—"

"You don't know anything about it! You told me yesterday you'd surely have it on today!"

"Mr. Turner said not to. Mrs. Troy—"

"Why did he say not to?"

"I don't know. You better ask Mr. Turner. Look, Mrs. Troy. Now don't you get scared, but the cops are in your apartment."

I hurried in. Hankins was seated before our desk in the living room. He was so absorbed in a batch of Jeff's canceled checks that he didn't notice me, or pretended he didn't.

"Mr. Hankins," I said, "I'm afraid you're wasting your time. We put the proof that we killed Mike Kaufman in our safety deposit box."

He turned calmly to look at me. "Now, Mrs. Troy," he said placidly, "your husband is an amateur detective. You know how these things are." He gave me a pleasant smile, then raised his voice to bellow, "Find anything, Bolling?"

The big detective lumbered in from the kitchen shaking his head.

"Good morning, Mrs. Troy," he said.

"Mr. Hankins," I asked, "what are you looking for in particular?"

"Nothing in particular. I just wanted to make sure that this stuff was yours."

"You mean you still think it might have been Kaufman's? Look, Mr. Hankins, this furniture belongs to us! Honest, Mr. Hankins!"

"We got to make sure, Mrs. Troy. Kaufman's things are still someplace in this house; they have to be. They never left here. We checked with every trucking company within a hundred miles of New York. We checked with everybody in this house and on this street. We checked with the cops who have this beat. Nobody saw any furniture go. It *didn't* go! It's still in this house, all right. But where the hell where?" I shrugged helplessly and Hankins went on. "And where, incidentally, is your husband?"

"He went out for a long walk," I said.

"Nice day for it," Hankins growled. "Come on, Bolling. The tenants in this house should be wide awake enough by now to answer a few questions."

Landlord Turner must have been lurking in the hall outside our apartment, waiting for the detectives' departure, for almost immediately after they had left me he was standing timidly in our doorway.

"I hope you'll forgive me for bothering you, Mrs. Troy," he said, his voice a cautious whisper and his eyes on the stairs the police had just ascended. "I wanted to see you."

"And I'm very anxious to see *you!*" I threw the door wide open and beckoned him into the room. "Mr. Turner, I understand that you've told Charley not to get us a lock."

"Yes. Yes, I did. That's what I wanted to see you about."

"But, for heaven's sake, why? We can't go on living here with our door unlocked! Do you want us to get murdered in our sleep?"

His little rabbit eyes widened with righteous horror as he gratefully seized upon the point I had made.

"Mrs. Troy, that's just it! I thought that maybe—well, after all that's happened—you wouldn't want to stay here any longer. You'd like to move out."

Knowing landlords, I said in sincere astonishment, "You mean you'd let us break our lease?"

"It wouldn't matter at all about your lease," he said eagerly. Much too eagerly. I gaped at him. Then he caught the surprise in my face and his voice, as he continued, was overly nonchalant. "Of course, ordinarily, I would hold a tenant to his lease. That's my policy. You understand. But in this case—well, this is different. Mr. Kaufman being murdered in your bathtub and left in your garden and everything—well, I wouldn't blame you if you wanted to move. I wouldn't try to hold you, not at all."

For a moment I stood silent, thinking wistfully of a new and shiny enameled tub in which no corpse had ever bathed and a garden where nothing but flowers had bloomed and an apartment minus Hankinses and Bollings.

"You could move out this afternoon," Turner was saying encouragingly. "There's an empty place in one of my other buildings and I know a mover who could take care of you."

I shook my head ruefully; I had remembered Jeff. His heart would break if he couldn't live, for at least a year, in his old speakeasy. And I had also remembered another thing, the police. Would Hankins consider my squeamishness a justifiable excuse to move out or merely an excuse? Our relationship with the detective was too strained to take the risk of seeming to run away.

"It's very thoughtful of you, Mr. Turner, to make this offer," I said, "but I imagine we'll be staying."

"You're making a big mistake!" There was an ominous, warning note in the little man's voice.

"A big mistake!" I said sharply. "Why do you say that?"

But Mr. Turner wouldn't explain. Instead, he seemed to think that our conversation was becoming too lengthy, for he quickly bowed and scraped his way out of our apartment.

By noon my growing concern over the landlord's visit was displaced by a growing concern over Jeff. I spent until five o'clock assuring myself that he had gone to the studio and had not been set into a concrete block and dropped into the Hudson River, all expenses paid by our neighbor, the killer. When he finally did appear, at five-thirty, I was so glad to see him that I shouted angrily, "Where the hell have you been?"

"Number 507 West Twelfth Street. Wasting my time."

"You didn't find Bruhl?"

"No," he said disconsolately.

"But you saw who got the letter, didn't you?"

"The letter wasn't delivered."

"But, Jeff, it had to be!"

"I stayed for the second delivery and the third. It didn't arrive."

"Darling, if you address a letter to Jacob Bruhl at 507 West Twelfth Street, that letter's going to get there. The United States mail is—well, it's the United States mail!"

"A nice tribute to the boys, Haila, but—"

"But nothing! Neither rain nor snow nor hail nor something shall stay these couriers from the swift something of their appointed meetings. You can't get around that, Jeff! Jacob Bruhl must have got his hands on that letter before the U.S. Mail did."

"How could he?" Jeff asked patiently. "I put the letter in the box. I jiggled the shutter in the approved manner. The letter went safely in."

"Then there's only one explanation," I said. "The whole thing's an inside job. The Postmaster General, he done it."

"Yeah," Jeff said. He laughed hollowly.

We ate a silent and dismal dinner out of the cans I had salvaged from our cottage in Connecticut. Tomato soup, then black bean soup, then succotash for the main course. For dessert I offered Jeff his choice of vegetable soup or two marshmallows. He picked the marshmallows and threw them at me. Not playfully.

The living room, where I had set the table, was cold and cheerless with the rain, that seemed by now to have settled down for another run of forty days and forty nights, splashing against our windowed wall and a whining wind twisting and blowing the anemic sumac tree in the garden.

The garden itself was a puddle. Such a puddle that, had the corpse been discovered there now, the news that he had been drowned would have come as a surprise to no one.

Jeff sat moodily watching the rain and smoking innumerable cigarettes. I sat watching Jeff. His spirits could stay dampened for only so long and I was wondering what turn his escape would take. He surprised me; the philosophical was not on my list.

"We're youth," he said. "Youth is resilient. Therefore we are resilient. Ten years from now we will look back and—"

I interrupted him. "If you say, 'Look back and laugh,' I'll crown you with this percolator. Oh, I might get over the murder. I might. But I'll never get over the fact that my home was once a speakeasy. Your speakeasy. Your horrible past staring me in the face night and day."

"Haila, the horrible past to which you refer had its moments of sordidness, yes. But there were also moments of high, lyrical beauty. Like the time—"

"If you tell me about the time, I'll—"

"Put that percolator down. This time is different. It had absolutely nothing to do with women. I merely saved a man who was attempting suicide by eating broken glass in what is now our bedroom. I sent him bravely, his formerly rounded shoulders squared, out to fight the world. Today he is one of America's greatest benefactors. He has alleviated more pain, suffering and—"

"He's head of the Salvation Army, no doubt!"

"Uh-uh. He's president of one of America's largest aspirin companies."

Fortunately for my husband, Anne Carstairs chose that moment to knock at the door. She stood dripping in the hallway, the glistening rain on her face making the bright, hard little smile seem even harder. Her voice was crisp and casual.

"I've been out all day long," she was saying. "Has anything gruesome happened?"

I shook my head. "Except for the police it's been lovely and quiet. Well, anyway, quiet. No more bodies, no more anything."

"Haila, I thought maybe you'd like to get away from the scene of the crime. Why don't you and Jeff come up and spend the evening with me?"

"We're just having coffee, Anne. Won't you have some?"

"But I'm soaking. I've got to change."

"Well, slip into something dry and decent and come back."

"All right." She started up the stairs and then stopped. I saw the quick way her shoulders tightened and her hands gripped at her sides. When she turned back to me the brightness was stripped from her face.

"Haila, I—Oh, damn it, I'm a sissy! But I can't, I just can't do it. I can't go up there by myself."

"Where's Scott?"

"At the League. As usual. Please, Haila, you and Jeff come up with me. I'll make coffee."

"Darling, coffee isn't essential. Of course we'll go with you. It's horrible going into an empty place alone nowadays."

"Yes," Anne said. "You can't count on empty places being empty any more."

I called Jeff and we started up the stairs, three abreast, Anne's unnecessarily loud and gay chatter as we climbed gave proof of her nervousness. At the next floor George Turner, his coat over his arm, waited for us to clear his landing before he began his descent. There was a

KELLEY ROOS   95

smiling, a mumbling of greetings, and a great profusion of nods as we passed him.

Anne was fumbling with her key in front of the door when I became aware of eyes watching us. I jerked up my head. Miss Charlotte Griffith was leaning over the banister. Her plump arms and shoulders and the smooth cap of snowy hair seemed to fade into nothingness in the pale light of the hallway, and her face, wreathed in a great smile, seemed to be suspended in the air above us.

Her eyes moved from me to Anne. "I thought it was Miss Franklin coming up, dear. I did want to talk to her so. I—Well, good night, dear."

She turned and disappeared into her room. In spite of the endearment and the pleasant friendliness, I felt for the first time what Anne Carstairs had been feeling all along. A camouflaged hostility, a silent waiting watchfulness around us. Was it only a coincidence that George Turner had been making his departure when we reached that floor, that Charlotte Griffith had been quietly leaning over the banister? Was it only my imagination that made me feel ears glued to doorways, eyes peeping through cracks all about us?

A short gasp from Anne snapped me out of my nervous coma. She had stepped just inside the room and was staring around her with a puzzled frown. It was a moment before I realized that the room in which we stood had been thoroughly, but tidily, ransacked. The evidence of it was minute but undeniable. Ends of bright-colored linens stuck out of not quite closed drawers, rugs and pictures were disarranged, the desk and the shelves of books were in subtle disarray.

"Mr. Hankins," Jeff announced, "must have paid you a call."

"The police? But why? Why all this?"

"They've been stymied by not being able to find anything of Kaufman's, or about Kaufman. They must be starting all over again."

"But I thought they were all through with Scott and me." She was crouched in front of the shelves, straightening the lines of books, "I thought we had convinced them that—"

Anne's voice trailed off. Her eyes were riveted on the book she had just pushed into place. I saw her stretch out her hand and pull it off the shelf, then flip open the title page. Instantly she closed it again and, almost furtively, thrust it back beside the others.

Jeff was standing beside her. "What is it, Anne?"

"Nothing! I just didn't recognize—for a moment—" She faltered and her lips trembled. Then, with a frightened bewilderment, she grasped the book again and thrust it into Jeff's hands. "Jeff, look! I—I don't know—"

I stood on tiptoe and peered over his shoulder. On the title page, in a scrawling, spidery hand, was written: *To Mike Kaufman, Christmas, 1938.*

Anne said, "I don't know how it came to be here. I've never seen it before. Scott—he must have borrowed it without my knowing."

Jeff was down on one knee now, methodically but rapidly going through the Carstairses' entire library. "But Scott told Hankins that he didn't know Kaufman at all. He said he'd never spoken to him."

"He didn't, Jeff! I'm sure he never had anything to do with him, nothing at all!" Dread was slowly creeping into her voice. "Jeff, what does it mean? If Scott did borrow it from Kaufman—that won't matter, will it? It needn't mean anything. You don't have to know a person very well or be connected with him in any way just to borrow a book! You could—" She stopped, fighting down her sudden hysteria.

Jeff stood up abruptly. His face was serious. "We'd better talk to Scott right away, Anne. Hankins didn't miss this; he couldn't have."

"But if he did see it, Jeff, what could he—"

"If we could see Scott before Hankins does, we might be able to help. Where is he, Anne?"

"At the Art Students League."

"All right, let's go."

As Jeff opened the street door, we saw the big black car swing to the curb and squeal to a stop. Jeff closed the door. "Cheese it, the cops," he said. "Get back in our place, quick!"

We stood inside our bedroom, close to the wall, and listened to Hankins pound into the house, pause for a moment just outside our listening-post, then start up the stairs. We waited until we heard him knocking at some door above us, then we slipped out into Gay Street.

Our taxi stayed on Seventh Avenue until it hit Times Square. Then it swerved onto Broadway. At Fifty-Seventh Street we turned east and pulled to a halt in front of the big smooth gray building. Jeff paid the driver, then had to run to catch up with Anne and me as we hurried up the long sweeping staircase inside.

After blundering into two life classes and being swiftly made to correct our errors, we located the illustration class. The large studio was filled with smock-coated artists peering over and around their easels. On a dais in the center stood two models, a young man and a young woman, dressed in evening clothes. The boy stood easily, one hand in his pocket, the other proffering a silver cigarette case to the girl. One of her hands drooped gracefully over it as she smiled up at him, her head thrown slightly back.

But you could tell from the glaze in their eyes, the strain in their smiles, and the sag in their extended arms that they were mentally and painfully clicking off the seconds until their next five-minute rest period was called.

Before we could locate Scott, a thin sandy-haired youth rose from a chair by the model's stand and tiptoed over to us, a questioning look on his face.

Jeff said, "We're looking for Scott Carstairs."

"Scott isn't at the League this year," Sandy said.

"He isn't—" Anne's voice rose so that at least half of the aspiring artists cast dirty looks in our direction. "But he is! He's in this class, this illustration class!"

"Look," Sandy said, "I know Scott Carstairs. He used to study here, two or three years ago. But he isn't here now."

"He—he must be!" Anne insisted.

Sandy shrugged and shook his head. "No." And then, as if he didn't care to argue the point further, he turned to the models. "All right, rest," he said. He moved over to the girl, leaving us looking at each other.

Anne said stammeringly, "He's got to be here. He—Don't you understand? He's got to be!" From where we stood, all three of us searched the room. There was no Scott Carstairs among the assembled artists. Anne, her eyes wide with incredulity, touched Jeff's arm. "See that young man over there—the blond with the glasses. He's lighting a cigarette now."

"Yes," Jeff said.

"He works with Scott at the agency. I don't know his name; Scott just pointed him out to me on the street once. Jeff, talk to him, will you? Ask him."

"Sure."

Jeff crossed the room to accost the young man with the glasses. Anne watched them anxiously, her eyes focused intently as if she were trying to read their lips. We saw Jeff pick up a pencil from among the artist's things and make a note on the back of an envelope. Then he came back to us.

"Well?" Anne demanded.

Jeff glanced down at the envelope, but Anne had already snatched it from his hand. " 'Revere,' " she read. " 'Twenty-Two Beekman Place.' " She raised her face to Jeff, her forehead wrinkled in puzzled lines.

"That's where Scott is."

"Why? Why is he there?"

"I don't know."

Anne set her lips firmly. "I'm going to Beekman Place. There's something the matter. Scott wouldn't have lied to me—he wouldn't unless—"

People were beginning to look at us. Jeff took Anne by the arm and led her out of the studio. No one spoke until we were on the sidewalk in front of the building.

"Please," she begged, "let's go there, right away. Scott's in trouble, I know he is!"

"Anne—" I started.

She hailed a cruising cab and we crawled into it. Anne sat between Jeff and me, her whole body rigid, her hands mechanically tearing the envelope in her lap into shreds.

Jeff said, "Look, Anne, there'll be some good reason for this. It's nothing to worry about. Scott must have—"

"We'll soon find out," she said quietly. "He's in trouble. We'll soon know what it is."

There were flower boxes in the windows of the house at 22 Beekman Place, two tall trees skirting its front wall, a tiny patch of yard on either side of the steps that led up to the simple, smart-looking door. Anne rang the bell beside it.

Almost immediately the door was opened by a woman. She was about forty, tall, and with a slinky slenderness. A trailing black velvet hostess gown wrapped itself clingingly around her graceful figure. Her ink-black hair was parted in the middle and swooped sleekly down over her ears to end in a heavy knot low on her neck. Her mouth was a wide vermilion slash across the ivory whiteness of her face.

"Revere?" Anne asked tremulously.

"Yes, I'm Mrs. Revere."

"I'm sorry to bother you. I—"

I saw what had happened to Anne's face even before her words had come to their fumbling stop. I saw the color drain from it, quickly and completely, as if a heavy roller had wrung it out. And then, over her shoulder, I saw the reason for it.

Scott Carstairs was lounging in a big chair in the living room upon which the front door opened. His coat was off, his tie hanging loose around his unbuttoned collar. He was more at home than I had seen him at 39 Gay Street. Ice flashed as he placed the highball glass he was holding on an end table and took a cigarette out of a box.

The half-choking sound came from Anne. Scott heard it and his eyes shifted to the doorway. His face became as white as hers as he hurried across the room and pushed past the woman in black.

"Anne," he said. "Anne—"

Anne looked at them both for a long silent moment. Then, without a word, she turned and ran down the street.

CHAPTER ELEVEN

WITH AN ANGRY, MUFFLED EXCLAMATION, Scott followed Anne through the rain. At the corner of Beekman Place, she jumped into a taxi, but before the napping driver had time to start the motor, Scott was climbing in beside her. We saw the cabbie slouch back in his seat again; evidently Scott had canceled his wife's flight orders.

Mrs. Revere, Jeff, and I stood helplessly, glancing furtively at each other. The situation, to say the least, was embarrassing. Our unexpected hostess tried out a small laugh that didn't quite come off. "Well—" she said tentatively.

That "well" broke enough ice for Jeff to find an opening. "Mrs. Revere," he said, "I'd like you to meet Mrs. Jeff Troy and her husband. We're friends of Anne Carstairs."

The white forehead wrinkled delicately, charmingly. "Anne?" she repeated, putting a question mark at the end.

"The pursued," Jeff explained. "Mrs. Scott Carstairs." He pushed his index finger in the direction of the taxi.

"Mrs. Carstairs! But I didn't know—I never guessed—" Mrs. Revere was both surprised and flustered. And both became her. The tinted eyelids opened wide, sweeping long, mascaraed lashes into a beautiful upward curve. Her small but full lips parted, revealing perfect, dazzling teeth.

"Please," she urged, "please, won't you come in?"

It was not only an invitation to an explanation, it was a command. She turned from us and led the way into the living room, the train of her velvet gown trailing behind her, pulling the cloth tight around her hips and thighs exactly as it was meant to. *Uh-huh*, I thought. *The woman of that interesting age that we younger wives are warned against.*

Mrs. Revere glided across the high-ceilinged beamed living room and thrust open one of the casement windows. She turned, paraded to the fireplace and made a picture there. One arm stretched full length along the mantelpiece with long fingers drooping languidly over the edge, the other arm crooked behind her. That did the right things to the right places. She kicked her train expertly so that the slit of her gown parted to her knee. *Uh-huh*, I thought again. *Anne knew what made Anne run.*

"Do sit down," Mrs. Revere said, presenting us with a charming smile. By now she was again the sleek, poised mannequin who had opened the door for us. Jeff and I mumbled in joint confusion and stood where we were. Then our hostess laughed, and there was sympathy and distress and understanding in it. We laughed, too, hollowly at best, but things were some better for it. At least we stopped shifting from feet to feet and dropped onto the gorgeous divan that stretched itself before the fireplace.

"It's all so very, very strange," Mrs. Revere began. "You see, I had no idea that Scott Carstairs was married. I can't understand why he never told me."

"Scott's modest," Jeff said. "Then again, maybe he didn't want to bother you with details."

Anger smoldered for a brief moment in her eyes, but as quickly was gone. "You think, of course—and she thinks—That's why the poor child fled!"

"I'd say so," Jeff said. "Look, Mrs. Revere. Haila and I—we wish we were someplace else. We're not surprised, though, to find ourselves here. When strange and nude corpses are delivered to your back door like a bottle of milk—well, after such things, you're shockproof."

"Oh! Then you're the people Scott's been talking about."

"Well, we're the people with the corpse. But we didn't come up here to snoop into Scott's private life. We went to the League, where we thought he'd be, to ask him a question. An important one. And we traced him here. And then Anne sees you—And well, what do you think she gathered when she found her only husband—Do you mind if I don't complete my sentences for a while yet?"

Mrs. Revere smoothed the already satin-smooth black hair with a distrait hand. "I don't seem to be able to think at all yet, Mr. Troy. It's all so amazing." She had forgotten about her poise now and was simply standing before us, puzzled and worried. Not nearly so alluring, but much nicer. "I think I can—well, look over there, please!"

She pointed to a large drawing-board propped on a table that was directly behind us. Three baby giant panda bears were being chased across the drawing-paper by a towheaded little boy.

I said, "Oh! You're—Are you *Maude* Revere?"

"Yes," she said, smiling. "Wee books for wee children. And Scott is illustrating the one I'm doing now."

It took a second or two for that to sink in. Jeff was the first to voice his comprehension. "You mean, Scott comes here and paints baby giant panda bears?"

"Exactly, Mr. Troy. If Anne will only come in and look at Mickey, Ickey, and Stickey, I'm sure everything will be fine again, won't it?"

"It ought to be," I said, "she should—"

Mrs. Revere's eyes lighted with a sudden mischievous glint. "In case you still have any doubts about Scott and me—" She raised her voice and called, "Brad! Are we disturbing you?"

She kept her smiling eyes on us as the pleasant male voice shouted back from another room. "Not a bit!" it said. "Is there someone there besides Scott?"

"Yes, but you needn't appear! Go on with your work." She spread her hands in a wide, comic gesture. "Friends—my husband!"

Jeff and I laughed with her, a sheepishly uproarious laugh.

"My husband writes, too," she went on, "but for adults. Political history. And now, Mr. and Mrs. Troy, are you completely convinced about Scott's and my relationship?"

"On all but one point," Jeff said. "Are you sure that your books are on the up and up? That they aren't subversive propaganda aimed to win our young over to some malignant foreign power?"

"Perhaps! I hope this one makes the kiddies all want to be panda bears instead of good American citizens."

"Hmm," Jeff said, "a secret agent of the animal kingdom."

"Exactly!" Maude Revere grinned delightfully, then grew serious. "But, really, I don't understand this. Scott and I have been working together for several months; he's up here nearly every night. Why he shouldn't have told me about his wife—or, stranger than that—why he hasn't told Anne about this! He must have given her *some* explanation for all the time—"

"Anne thought he was studying at the League."

"But why?" The bafflement we all felt showed most clearly on Maude Revere's expressive face. "Why should he do that? He hasn't only been doing work for me, you know. He's done lots of other things, jobs I've helped arrange for him myself. Illustrating books, designing jackets, posters—"

"All things he had to do at night?" Jeff asked.

"Yes."

"But he didn't want Anne to know about them. He told her he was studying."

Maude Revere said thoughtfully, "Scott's always refused to sign his work with his own name. He thought the agency might not like it. But perhaps all along it was because of Anne—"

She covered up hastily, for Scott was stamping back into the room. His face was flushed with angry frustration, his hands worked nervously at his sides.

Mrs. Revere planted herself in front of him. "Where's Anne, Scott? Why didn't you bring her in with you?"

"She wouldn't come," he said. "She's gone home."

"But, Scott, you told her! You didn't let her think—"

"I tried to tell her. She wouldn't listen."

Maude Revere's hands went to her cheeks in horror. "Scott! She still believes that you and I—"

"Yes." His voice was quietly furious. "She wouldn't let me talk to her. And now—I don't give a damn what she thinks."

"Stop it! You've no right to be angry with her. She *should* be hurt and confused. What else can you expect? You've lied to her and—"

"All right, Mrs. Revere. I've lied to her."

"Why?"

"I'm afraid it's none of your business." There was no anger left in him now. This was only a statement of fact. His eyes moved to Jeff and me. "And it's none of your business, either. None of your damn business, I might add. If you hadn't followed me—"

"We didn't follow you, Scott," Jeff said. "At least, not for the reason you think. For this reason, in your apartment there's a book that belonged to Mike Kaufman. His name is on the title page. The cops have found it; they ransacked your place this afternoon."

Scott laughed. "What's the difference? I borrowed a book from the man. I met him on the stairs one day and he had it with him. He loaned it to me and I forgot to return it. What's strange about that?"

"Nothing. Except I'm afraid that Hankins will remember that you said you'd never spoken to Mike Kaufman."

"I forgot about that. It was the only time I ever did, and I forgot about it."

"I see." Jeff looked at him out of the corner of his eye. "What was the book you borrowed, Scott?"

"I don't even remember," Scott said, closing the subject.

After a moment Jeff said, "I'm sorry about this."

"It doesn't matter," Scott told him and walked away to the casement window.

With Scott ignoring us and with Maude Revere making soft apologies at our side, we finally managed to get out of the house.

In the taxi, homeward bound, I said miserably, "Jeff, Scott might have really borrowed that book. And forgotten about it. It isn't impossible."

"Fairly impossible."

"Why?"

"The name of that book, Haila, was *Butterfield 8*. And in the Carstairs bookcase there's another book, with Scott's name in it, and the title of that book is *Butterfield 8*. Why in hell should he borrow a copy of a book he already owns?"

"Oh, Jeff! And do you think Hankins saw that other book, the second one?"

"Sure. That's why I hoped Scott would have a better story than the one he gave me."

We rode the rest of the trip in silence. The cab pulled up in front of 39 Gay Street, and we got out. There was light streaming from the Carstairses' front windows, streaming—with nice irony—cheerfully.

And I thought of Anne up there alone. I thought of how I would be feeling if—

"Jeff," I said, "we can probably explain to Anne more easily than Scott can. She'll listen to us."

He shook his head firmly. "I've done enough messing around in other people's lives for one night. It's a record, even for me."

"We'll be helping."

"Not with *my* delicate touch."

"She's all alone, Jeff, she needs someone."

"I think it would be nice for Anne if you went up. Why don't you?"

"I think I will. What are you going to do?"

"Wrack my brains. About a bedridden lady and her sister. About another lady who has a restaurant and a small boy. About a man named Jacob Bruhl who doesn't get the letters you write to him. About Mike Kaufman. Furniture. A gangster named Ziggy Koehler and a landlord. A retired art dealer. Scott Carstairs and a borrowed book."

"I know Scott hasn't anything to do with all of this!"

"Panda bears," he went on, "doors opening and closing in the middle of the night. Screens with addresses on them, this and that. Thirty-Nine Gay Street. *Toujours gai* Street."

Jeff slammed into the bedroom, and I started up the stairs.

I hadn't made up my mind what to expect in Anne's apartment, but what I found was a distinct shock. Anne, bright-eyed, dry-eyed, with a hard, tight smile on her lips. Anne, freshly made up, wearing a dark-blue suit. On the couch was a half-packed suitcase. She was carrying an armful of clothes toward it.

"Anne," I said, "you're not—"

"I'm taking a little trip, Haila. I've got an old friend in Baltimore who's been begging me for years to visit her. So I thought I'd run down now and—"

"Anne, you can't! You mustn't!"

"I'm just dying to meet her new husband. She writes me that they're so much in love. You know how young married couples are. So idealistic, so true to each other!"

"Anne, do you know who Mrs. Revere is?"

"Yes. A very beautiful woman."

"She's Maude Revere, the children's author. And Scott's illustrating her new book for her."

Anne dropped the clothes she was holding and turned to me. "She's—Oh, Haila—"

"It's true, Anne. Scott's done several books for her. And to show you how utterly silly you've been; he does them while Mr. Revere works on some historical tome in the next room." Anne sat down slowly, looking at me with wide-eyed suspicion. "Scott's been doing just what you've known he was doing. Breaking his neck to make money, that's all. I thought you should know that, Anne, before you did anything. It's the truth. And now that I've played my self-appointed role of Mrs. God, I will awkwardly withdraw."

"Thanks, Haila," a quiet voice said from the doorway. It was Scott. He closed the door and took a few steps toward Anne. "It's true, darling. That's exactly the way it is."

"Why didn't you tell me, Scott? Instead of lying to me all this while, instead of making me think you were at the League?"

"I—I wanted to surprise you."

"Oh, Scott!" There was a sob in Anne's voice. "You've been letting me sit here night after night in order to surprise me! No surprise that money could buy would make up for that. The way we've scraped and budgeted and done without things, without fun. Without each other, even! What were you going to surprise me with, Scott? A yacht? A house at Aiken?"

"You don't believe me?" Scott asked grimly.

"I want to believe you! I want so much to believe you, but—Scott, why?"

"Anne," he said miserably, "you've got to—" He stopped and his face hardened. "I can't tell you anything. Nothing at all. Only—Anne, try to trust me, darling."

"I have been trusting you."

"I know." His eyes faltered before her steady gaze and he looked away. He saw the suitcase on the divan. "You're leaving?"

"I thought I might."

"No." He crossed the room to her quickly, put his hands on her shoulders. "Anne, please stay here. Some day I can explain everything. Soon, I hope. Just now all I can tell you is—"

"Is what?"

"That I love you, Anne." He moved closer to her. "You mustn't go away. If you leave now, after this murder, after all that's happened here—"

Anne took a slow step backward. Her whole body was rigid. "I see. If I leave you now, the police might think—" She hesitated and her eyes filled with horror. "Scott!"

"Anne, what are you thinking?" He forced a laugh. "Darling, I didn't kill that man! You don't—you can't be thinking that!"

She sat on the couch and buried her face in her hands. "No, I don't think that. But I—I don't know what to believe now. My whole world has—it's fallen apart, Scott, it's—"

There was no time to answer the imperative tattooing, for the door was opening before it had even stopped, and Lieutenant Detective Hankins stepped into the room. His eyes were grimly triumphant as they rested on Scott.

"I thought you'd never show up, Carstairs," he said. "Suppose we have a little talk now, just you and I. Mrs. Carstairs, you can busy yourself in some other room, can't you? And I'm sure it's past your bedtime, Mrs. Troy."

CHAPTER TWELVE

I RAN DOWN THE STAIRS to our apartment, where I brought Jeff up to date on the police developments and then we waited, nervously and for a long time, until we heard Hankins's heavy tread in descent. From our window we watched him climb into the black car and drive down the little winding street. He had been alone.

"So," I said in relief, "he hasn't got enough on Scott to do anything about him."

"You like Scott, don't you, Haila?"

"Well, Anne's my pal, and she likes Scott. She loves him. That's good enough for me. Scott doesn't have any connection with this murder; he couldn't have."

"Because Anne's your pal and she loves him. Fine logic! Haila, there are days when you wear your heart in your head and your mind on your sleeve. I ought to divorce you."

"I'm positive," I insisted, "that there's some perfectly innocent reason for Scott's behavior. Jeff, you don't think that he—that he killed Mike Kaufman?"

"I'm not permitting myself the dubious pleasure of any mental accusations, sweetheart. Scott could have done it, even if Anne does love him. Lucy Griffith could have done it, even if her sister Charlotte loves her. Nobody loves Mr. Turner—or Henry Lingle, as far as I know—but that doesn't mean that one of them *did* do it."

"Stop kidding me!" I lifted my foot to kick him gently in the shins, but as his right hand changed into a right fist I changed my mind. "It's a good thing for you," I went on, "that I am sentimental and loyal. Because when I'm logical about you, Jeff, I—well, frankly, I wonder why."

"Why what?"

"Why I find you so non-repulsive."

"I'm non-repulsive," Jeff said. "Non-repulsive. I try and try and try. I spend thousands on personal appearance. I do without lunches to have a hot towel and I—Haila, let's have a drink. In the garden."

"The garden? Jeff, it's been raining all day."

"Look, Haila." He drew me to the bedroom window and pointed through the top pane. In the sky thin clouds were racing out of the way of the moon, clearing the stage for it. "See," Jeff said, "it'll be beautiful in the garden. Moonlight will catch the raindrops as they fall from our sumac tree and change them into pearls. We'll stand enchanted. Or if you're too tired to stand enchanted, I'll drag out some chairs. And the coffee table."

"Um-hum," I said squeamishly. "Put my chair right on the spot where Mike Kaufman was found."

"Darling, we've got to use our garden; we can't let it go to waste forever. Listen, when a pilot crashes they send him back up in another plane immediately—"

"Oh, I'll go out in *another* garden."

Jeff startled me by abruptly flinging open the window and shouting, "Hey, Miss Franklin!"

Polly halted on the first of the three steps that led down into the entrance of number 39. "Hiya, Mr. Troy," she said, grinning. "Why the Miss? Is your wife at home? Oh, hello, Haila."

"Polly," Jeff said, "come in and have a drink with us."

"I'll come in but I don't want a drink. And I don't want to talk murder, either. I'm too tired."

We escorted Polly into our apartment and through it to the garden. The moon was high enough in the sky now to have center stage and was playing its part to the hilt, and in its soft yellow glow the garden didn't look so bad. While Polly and Jeff dragged chairs and a table from the living room I went into the kitchen and took an inventory of our liquor supply.

A cocktail, I decided, in spite of the hour, would be the light touch that might turn our minds away from the past and toward the future. And I would mix one for Polly against her changing her mind.

After pouring rum, grenadine, lemon juice, and ice into the tall chromium shaker, I wrapped it in a tea towel and delivered it to Jeff in the garden. While he gave it the shaking, I collected three glasses from the china closet that had been built into the defunct fireplace in our middle room.

Polly slipped the palm of her hand flat over the glass as Jeff bent to pour her cocktail. "None for me, Jeff, really. At the restaurant I have to be polite and accept drinks. Actually, I hate the stuff."

Jeff filled my glass, then his. "I hate it, too," he said. "Because of what it's done to Haila."

"Mine is a tragic case, indeed!" I scoffed. "One cocktail before dinner, that's me."

"Haila can't eat on an empty stomach," Jeff explained. "There! Look at the moonlight on those raindrops! Pearls, I told you."

"You could do things with this garden," Polly said, looking around. Then she added, laughing, "But I'm not sure what. Go ahead, drink, you two."

"Yes, Jeff, when I spend hours bending over a cold cocktail shaker, you might at least—"

Because I was speaking I didn't hear it as soon as the others did. It was their eyes, leaping up the back wall of the house, that made me break off and listen. A woman's voice grew louder and louder, rising toward hysteria. Then a scream cut like a knife through the quiet night. It was a scream that made me shudder and grasp the sides of my chair, that made Polly Franklin wince as if she had been slashed across the face with a whip, that made Jeff grit his teeth. Then it died away into tearing, fearful whimpers. There was a scuffling sound high above our heads.

"It's Lucy," Polly said. "Lucy Griffith."

Jeff ran through the French doors and right up and over the love seat that was between him and the middle room. Getting out into the hallway slowed him up enough for me to catch him. I was at his heels as he raced up the three flights of steps to the Griffiths' floor.

He pounded on the door. The sobbing seemed more remote now than it had when we stood in our garden. It was no more than a broken moaning, exhausted and beaten. There was no other sound in the room but that.

Jeff was beating at the door now, kicking at it, calling out Lucy Griffith's name. For ten seconds he kept at it. Polly, breathing hard from the exertion of her quick climb, had reached the landing and stood help-lessly beside us.

"Break it down, Jeff," I said. "Break it open!"

He stepped back, hunched his shoulders, and lunged. He was already in motion and unable to check himself, although all three of us saw that the door had started to open. Jeff hit it and shot right on into the living room as the door swung around on its hinges. He went crashing to the floor at Charlotte Griffith's feet.

Miss Griffith stood looking down at him, her plump hands clenched at her sides, her eyes narrowed with anger. Then, instantly, she had relaxed. Her face had folded into its usual friendly, slightly worried smile and she was clumsily assisting Jeff to his feet.

"We heard her scream," Jeff said. "We thought your sister—"

Miss Griffith inclined her head toward the open door at the side of the room. I could see just the edge of a rumpled bed and a table littered with sickroom supplies. A glass half filled with water, bottles, teaspoons, together with a small portable radio and an opened book, stacked the table perilously high. A tiny, wasted hand stretched out from the bed even as I looked, and fell listlessly across the book.

"Lucy had a—one of her attacks," Charlotte Griffith was saying. "The police, their endless questions and their prying have upset her. They drove her into hysterics. She's all right now, Mr. Troy. I've given her a sedative, she'll be all right now."

As she talked she was moving toward us, her great bulk seeming to surround and envelop us and push us toward the hall. The friendly smile never left her face, her voice was serene and soft. And yet she drove us out of that room as effectively as if she had been armed with a cat-o'-nine-tails. The door closed gently in our faces. The bolt behind it slid into its socket.

Jeff turned to Polly. She shrugged her broad shoulders and put her hands on her forehead.

"I don't know," she said. "And, damn it, I don't care. Good night." She started up the stairs.

"You'd better have that drink now, Polly."

"No, thanks. I'm going to bed and hide my head under the covers until—until forever."

We waited until she had disappeared around the bend in the stairs, then Jeff took me by the arm and guided me down to our place and through it to the garden.

"No, dear," I said. "All of a sudden that garden appeals even less to me. I need a drink, but I'll have it here in the living room."

Sitting opposite each other in our love seats, we found ourselves speechless, still stunned. The explanation which Charlotte Griffith had given us for that series of bloodcurdling screams was distinctly unsatisfying. And yet I could find no other explanation. Jeff evidently felt the same way. He heaved a baffled sigh, shook his head hopelessly, and picked up his glass.

"Haila," he said with obvious distaste, "what is this I am about to drink?"

"It's a Bacardi. Why?"

"It's a funny color."

"I mightn't have put enough grenadine in it. I don't like them too sweet."

"Would it undermine your confidence as a bartender," he asked, "if I had a rye and soda?"

"Not at all. You're so charming about it."

"You usually make things too sweet, and now suddenly you—"

"I've changed, Jeff. I'm not getting any younger, you know."

"Haila, I just happen not to like—"

"Oh, go get your rye and soda. Put some sugar in it."

A moment later he was back from the kitchen, taking healthy pulls on his highball and eyeing my cocktail with mild loathing. I didn't want it any more myself, but I could hardly give Jeff the satisfaction of knowing that. Holding it to the light, I said, "How lovely! Darling, I'm going to let you have one sip. Just one, no more."

I touched the brim of my glass lightly to his lips and he averted his head with a grimace. I laughed at him and opened my mouth to show him what a girl could do with a properly concocted Bacardi.

I saw his right hand come up from the floor, but I couldn't do a thing about it. It hit the glass, knocking it clear across the room where it splintered against the wall. My cocktail was soaking slowly through my blouse and freezing my skin. Jeff sat staring at me, his lower lip clenched between his teeth, his eyes glazed.

"Jeff," I sputtered, "is the insanity in your family finally—"

"Haila! Darling—" He gulped, he shook his head, he tried to speak and couldn't. Then, suddenly, in a squeaking voice, he said, "Poison."

"Poison! You—you tried to poison me and you lost your nerve—"

I stopped. The bottom had fallen out of my voice. Then the bottom fell out of the rest of me as I realized what had almost happened. The shakes that started in my fingers wound up at last in the springs of the love seat. Jeff grabbed me by both shoulders and held me tight.

I said, "I'm all right, Jeff, I'm fine. Uh—thanks for being so insistent about my not drinking that—uh—poison. I like it, you know, but it doesn't like me."

"I would have missed you, Haila."

"I would have missed you, too, Jeff."

"Promise me you'll give up that type of drinking. I'm not nearly finished with you yet. Get a little older first."

"I'm so glad I married a man who knows poison when he smells it. I'll never regret it."

Jeff picked up his untouched cocktail and sniffed.

"More of the same," he said. "The funeral was to be double."

"What is it? Cyanide, Paris green, arsenic?"

"I don't know."

"Maybe it isn't poison at all."

Jeff unscrewed the top of the shaker and smelled its dark interior. "There's none of it in this thing. So that stuff was put in our drinks after they were poured."

"After they were poured," I repeated. "Jeff! While we were up at the Griffiths'!"

He nodded. "It had to be done then. Unless Polly managed it before the scream."

"Polly!" I exclaimed. "No, Jeff, she couldn't have. Not without us noticing. Besides—"

"Besides," Jeff finished for me, "Polly is such a nice person. It doesn't have to be Polly. It could have been anyone in the whole house. Except Charlotte Griffith, of course."

"Why?"

"We were on the next to the top floor. Everybody—the Carstairses, Lingle, Turner, Polly—all of them were between us and our drinks."

"Yes."

"It could even have been a trick—that scream—to get us away from those drinks."

"Yes," I said slowly, "but if it was, what does it mean? Who knew we were having them except Polly? And how could she know we were going to invite her in? There are so many questions—"

"Anybody could have looked out a back window and seen us in the garden. So anyone could have known where to put the poison."

"The question I'd really like an answer to is who. And why? And is he going to try again?"

"The who is the same person who opened our door last night. And the why must be that we're messing up his murder for him and he wants us out of the way. Maybe he's afraid we'll learn something we shouldn't. Or have already. About trying again—well, it's not likely he'll try again tonight. He won't know until tomorrow morning that we didn't drink the stuff and are, consequently, still alive."

"What a house!" I groaned. "Darling, let's get out of here!"

"Where would we go?" Jeff asked absently, not even considering the possibility of making an exodus. He carefully carried his cocktail into the kitchen. I watched him rinse out a nearly empty French dressing bottle and pour the poisoned Bacardi into it. "This," he said, "I will turn over to Hankins like the loyal citizen that I am. And now, sweetheart, let's go to bed and get some sleep. Tomorrow will be a busy day."

"Do you think I could sleep after being nearly done to death by a—"

"Darling," Jeff said, slipping his arm around me, "nothing's going to happen, we'll be all right. So listen. Until tomorrow morning we're going to forget that we even live at thirty-nine Gay Street. We're going to pretend we still live uptown, that we've never met any of the people who live in this house or who have died in this house. Is it a bargain?"

"It's a pleasure. For tonight we are somebody else someplace else."

I crawled into bed beside Jeff, propped up my pillow, fixed my lamp, and opened my book. For a while all the words seemed to begin with a *B* as in Bacardi, but eventually my nerves quieted enough for me to make a fair pretense at reading.

Jeff's return to normalcy came at approximately the same time as mine. Just as I was really becoming interested in my book he raised himself on one elbow.

"Are you going to read all night?" he snapped with his usual forced irritability.

"Just let me finish this one page, Jeff," I pleaded.

"Is it big print or small?"

"Big. Biggest print I've ever seen."

"Well, all right, finish the page, then. On one condition. Don't do any reading between the lines." He rolled over muttering, "As soon as I can afford it I'm going to have you learn Braille."

I finished the page, reading the last word twice in a silent revolt against Jeff's tyranny, and snapped off the light.

It was the draft that awoke me and sat me up shivering and chattering in the darkness. A minor gale, cold and tingling, was cutting straight across our bed, making its way toward some left-open window in the back of the house. That, I thought sleepily, must be remedied at once. Drafts cause neuralgia, stiff necks, and pneumonia. I swung my feet onto the floor and reached for my dressing gown. And then I heard the sound—a rustling, scraping noise—over by the open bedroom window.

A dog or a cat or an inebriated passerby was lolling outside the window. Barefooted, I paddled across the room to scat whatever it was away. Two steps from Mr. Turner's screen I halted. The sound had been repeated, but this time I knew it was no passerby outside. There was someone behind that screen—and in our room.

I took a quick step backward and opened my mouth to call for Jeff. Then, without warning, the screen rose in the air and flew at me. Simultaneously there was a rush of footsteps across the room to the hall door. I was too involved with the screen to do anything but screech.

"Haila—" Jeff called in a sleep-drunken voice.

"Somebody—the hall!" I gasped.

Jeff rolled across the bed and started for the door. His foot got tangled in the sheet that was trying to follow him and, to the accompaniment of a curse that nearly lit up the room, he sprawled full length on the floor. He was up again in a second and out into the hall.

I chased after him but stopped at the door. The hallway outside was completely dark, the stairway, the landings above, all plunged in blackness. I couldn't see a thing, not even my husband.

"Jeff!" I whispered.

Somewhere not far from me I heard his voice. "Where in hell is the damn wall bracket?" Then there was a click, another click, but no light.

"Haila, switch on the bed lamp!"

I was already feeling for it. I pulled the little chain and waited while nothing happened. Jeff was at my elbow now.

"Damn it!" he said. "They've blown out the fuse for the whole house."

"Jeff!" I had suddenly realized that he wasn't standing beside me any longer. "Jeff, where are you?"

His whisper and a creaking on the staircase came at the same time. "I'm going up. I'm going to find out who—"

"No!"

"Shh! Stay where you are, Haila."

I groped my way to him and clutched his arm. "Jeff, no! He might be waiting for you up there. Please—don't take a chance!"

"Ouch! Take your fingernails out of me! Go back into the bedroom and—"

"I'm coming with you."

I heard him groan in resignation and then, unwilling to waste time in argument, he found my hand and we started feeling our way up the stairs, climbing quietly and with great caution.

I drew each breath and took each step with loving care, knowing that it might be my last. My neck ached from the way I held my head when I expected a crowbar or its equivalent to come crashing down upon it. There was no sound except for the pattering of our bare feet and the pittering of my heart which, at the moment, also felt bare.

At the top of the first flight I reached out my hand to find the landing banister and another hand touched mine. I didn't scream; there was something in the touch that made me realize this hand held no threat or menace. It was tiny and feeble and caught at me pleadingly.

"Who is it?" I whispered.

"Mrs. Troy—it is you, isn't it?"

"It's both of us," Jeff said.

"I heard you downstairs. I thought it must be. I wanted to see you, Mr. Troy. I—I had to see you. I've got to talk to you."

"Who is it?" I asked again.

"I'm Lucy Griffith."

Jeff said, "Come downstairs with us, Miss Griffith, and—"

"No! No, I mustn't!" Fright leaped into the small, quavering voice. "No, I can tell you here. I shouldn't tell you. I may have to go back if I do and then I'll die. I don't seem to care though. That's what I keep telling her, that I don't care. That I'd rather die back there than go on with this."

"To go on with what?" Jeff asked gently.

"Murder. I won't be dragged into a murder. I keep telling her that but she won't listen. I tell her that to steal—well, that's bad, of course—only sometimes you have to and then it doesn't matter so much. But killing—I can't—I don't know what to do. I want somebody to tell me what to do."

The beam of light shot straight down the stair well. It flicked along our landing, then caught Lucy Griffith's face in its glare. It was the same pinched, childish face that I had seen pressed against the window the night we had moved in. But now, with the blinding light full on it, I could see its pallor and its thinness, the bloodless lips and great staring eyes with dark hollows under them.

From above us came Charlotte Griffith's voice, shaking with alarm.

"Lucy! Lucy, darling! What are you doing?"

The big woman stood on the landing of the fourth floor, the flashlight in her hand still beating down on Lucy's upturned face. Behind it, in the upward glow, Charlotte's was contorted with sisterly worry. She waddled down the stairs with amazing rapidity, the voluminous folds of her bathrobe dragging behind. She was breathing heavily when she reached Lucy and put an arm around her trembling shoulders.

"Darling!" The voice was crammed with quiet reproach. "Darling, you shouldn't do this, you mustn't. You aren't well, you know. Come, now, Lucy, back we go! Here, I'll help you, dear. We'll get you tucked back in bed now."

It was as though she were talking to a small child, wheedling it gently into submission. For a moment, Lucy drew back, shaking her head and protesting. Then, with a resigned sigh that was almost a gasp, she allowed her sister to half guide, half carry her up the stairs.

They had reached their doorway when, as if by some telepathic signal, the whole house awoke. Polly Franklin's door opened and Polly was leaning over the balustrade and swearing with sleepy abandon. I heard Anne Carstairs's anxious questions and Scott's reassurances. Henry Lingle's voice came from his doorway, bewildered and only half awake. George Turner was clumping down to the cellar to repair the short circuit. The house was alive with mutterings and confusion.

It was all over when, a few minutes later, the lights came on again.

Voices died down, doors closed, and 39 Gay Street, to all outward appearances, was sound asleep again.

CHAPTER THIRTEEN

"I KNOW I'M A CHUMP," Jeff admitted unhappily to Hankins on the detective's second visit that day. "The killer practically in bed with me and I let him get away."

Hankins banged his fist down on our table, making the lunch dishes dance. "The minute you figured that he was gunning for you, the minute you found that stuff in your cocktail, you should have sent for me. If I'd been here with some of my men it would have been a cinch."

"If you'd been here with some of your men," Jeff said, "we wouldn't have been visited by the murderer. He lives here; nothing goes on in this house that he isn't aware of. You don't think you could have sneaked four or five cops in here without him knowing about it, do you?"

"Frankly, Troy," Hankins said, "I don't know what to think."

"Toughest case of your career, huh, Mr. Hankins?" Jeff asked cheerfully. The way the detective glowered made him hurry on. "It's hard enough trying to find out who killed a known victim. But who killed whom! Well, I don't blame you at all for being stymied, Mr. Hankins."

"Thanks, Mr. Troy," he said sarcastically, "that makes me feel a lot better."

"If only Kaufman hadn't been stripped," Jeff said. "No clothes to trace back to their source, then forward again. That's what makes it so tough."

"The corpse," Hankins growled, "wasn't meant to be identified. And it hasn't been."

"Wasn't there anything at all? No distinguishing dental work? No old operations, tattooing, varicose veins, enlarged pores, tired, aching feet, spots before the eyes—"

"Nothing! Nothing that led any place. Pictures of Kaufman have been sent out, descriptions of him broadcast—the whole damn routine. And all we've drawn so far is a big blank."

"The gentleman," Jeff said, "was nobody. The furniture was chocolate, and the murderer ate it."

"It looks that way." Hankins paced off the length and width of our living room. He stopped in front of me. "Mrs. Troy, you were so close to the murderer or whoever it was last night that you must have noticed something about him."

"But I didn't," I insisted for the fourteenth time. "It was pitch-dark and there was a screen between us."

"Damn the man's modesty," Jeff said.

"Oh," Hankins said quickly to me, "you were able to see that it was a man, then. Not a woman. But you weren't able to see if the man was tall or short or old or—"

"Listen," Jeff shouted. "I'm the one who said *man*. And I didn't mean it literally. You yourself keep referring to the killer as *he*."

"I'm talking to your wife," Hankins snapped.

I picked up my cue. "I couldn't tell whether it was a man or a woman, Mr. Hankins. But if it was a woman, she was a very, very strong baby. That screen was thrown at me like a baseball."

"I bet," Hankins said pointedly, "that if I'd been in your place I'd have seen a little more."

"Maybe," I said, "but—"

"Hey," Jeff said, "are you implying that—"

"Go on, Troy."

"That there wasn't anyone in our room last night? That we weren't poisoned? That the whole thing's a trick?"

"Well, now that you mention it, Troy," Hankins cut in pleasantly, "I might be implying that. I've got plenty of reason to. First, you come out with that wacky story about Kaufman's phone call. Which gives you a nice alibi for the murder. Then this business in the dark last night and the murderer out to get you. Which certainly makes you look innocent.

And then a tale about a poisoned cocktail—which wasn't poisoned."

"Which wasn't—what?" I gasped.

"Wasn't poisoned," Hankins repeated serenely. "It was analyzed this morning. There was a big dose of sodium amytal in it, and that's all. It would have put the two of you sound asleep, all right, but not forever."

"Therefore," Jeff said angrily, "we put the stuff in the cocktails ourselves! The whole damn thing is a frame, is that it?"

"Tell me this, Troy, why would anyone who wanted to kill you put a sleeping-powder in your drink? The whole thing's screwy."

"Not so screwy," I said. "It's perfectly obvious to me. The killer didn't want Jeff to disturb him while he was polishing me off—or vice versa. Then, with one done, he could take care of the remaining Troy at his leisure."

"Nice fast thinking, Mrs. Troy. All right, just for the sake of argument, let's say the murderer is out to get you. Why?"

"He probably thinks that we know too much," Jeff said.

Hankins pounced. "And so do I! But what is it? What are you holding out?"

"Nothing!"

"You know who Mike Kaufman is, Troy!"

"Not that again," Jeff pleaded. "Look, Mr. Hankins. I never saw Kaufman before the other night. Everything that we've told you is true."

"Even the story about Lucy Griffith on the stairs last night?"

"Certainly. Have you talked to her about it?"

"Not yet. I've been up there twice but she's been sleeping each time. And she looked so done in that I decided to wait. But her sister says," Hankins's voice took a turn for the ominous, "that Lucy couldn't have talked the way you say she did. That you two must have dreamed the whole thing up."

"But she did!" I insisted. "I was there, I heard what she said."

"She might have been hysterical or sleepwalking," Jeff said, "but we gave you her very words."

Hankins shook his head. "Nothing you've told me since this case began has made any sense. Not a thing. I'm going to give you a little while longer. And then if you don't start making sense—"

He didn't finish his sentence. Looking enigmatically from Jeff to me, he stalked out of the room.

I took a deep breath.

"Why doesn't he arrest us, Jeff?"

"Don't be impatient, Haila. Give him a little more time. And give us a little more rope. We're doing all right. I think we'll get arrested."

"Jeff, seriously, do you think that?"

"Uh-uh, of course not," he said, and it was the most unconvincing noise I'd ever heard. "Haila, just a sleeping-powder. A mere Mickey Finn. I didn't save your life, Haila."

"No. All you did was cheat me out of a good night's sleep. And how I could have used one!"

"But why were we given a sedative?" Jeff puzzled. "An overdose of sedative? Why weren't we supposed to be waking up last night?"

The questions, I knew, were purely rhetorical; Jeff wasn't even considering the possibility of my answering them. And he was right. While he sat there in a one-man huddle, my mind went back to our narrow escape of the previous night. No matter what Hankins believed, our visitor had not been there for our health.

A person, I thought, *needs an evening like that occasionally to make her appreciate life*. Life is all right; it's a fine thing. In comparison with its alternative, it is absolutely dandy. There should be more of it.

Jeff jumped out of his chair and started for the door. I stepped in front of him.

"Where are you going, Jeff?"

"Up to have a chat with Polly Franklin."

"Then I'm going with you. I won't stay here alone."

"Haila, why don't you go to some seaside resort for a couple of weeks? Lie in the soothing sand, bask in the healing sun—"

"And read in the newspaper how the murderer gave you your lumps? No, thanks. I want to see you get your lumps. Let's go."

Polly received us in a pair of dark blue silk pajamas. Barefooted, no dressing gown, no makeup. Her hair couldn't have been touched by a comb or brush, but it looked wonderful. In one hand she held a glass of milk, in the other an apple. The crowded room was littered as before with newspapers and magazines, empty glasses, ashtrays, and articles of clothing.

We caught Polly's brother just about to take off for a business appointment. When we entered he flattered us by seeming to want to stick around. But Polly spiked that neatly.

"Run along, Ward," she said. "Business as usual. The Troys won't mind."

"Not at all," I said. "We'll be seeing you again, Mr. Franklin."

"I'm afraid you will. I'm not leaving town until this—this mess is cleared up."

"My big brother!" Polly laughed. She pushed him out into the hall and slammed the door. Then she waved us into seats and plopped herself down on the big bed, her legs crossed tailor-fashion. She expertly balanced the glass of milk on one knee while she used two hands to eat her apple.

"How's Bobby?" Jeff asked.

"Swell. I was just writing my daily report to him while I had breakfast. Or lunch or whatever you call it. Hey, I've got another apple. You two can split it. No? Would you like some tea?"

Jeff laughed at her. "What if we would?"

She grinned back. "I'd borrow some from the Misses Griffith." She threw her apple core toward a wastebasket, finished her milk, and then, leaning back on one elbow, yawned luxuriously. "What do you think people are going to want to eat tonight? I've got to phone a menu to the chef."

"Polly," Jeff said, "I'd like to talk to you about last night."

"Poor Lucy," Polly said.

"What exactly is wrong with Lucy?"

"If anyone thinks he has a tough life," Polly said, "let him take a look at those two sisters. I don't know which one I pity more. Lucy who is sick, or Charlotte who has to take care of her."

"What's wrong with Miss Lucy?" Jeff asked again.

Polly shrugged and dismissed the subject. She threw back her head and laughed, a full, hearty laugh. "You know, the silliest thing happened at the restaurant the other night—"

There was a knock at the door, and it was opened so immediately that Polly's shouted "come in" was superfluous. The newcomer was Henry Lingle, and at first glance I couldn't tell whether he was perturbed at finding Polly with visitors or merely surprised to see who the visitors were. But I soon realized that I was wrong on both counts; Henry Lingle was angry.

And he grew angrier as he spoke. "I've just been through another session with Hankins! This one is the last! Because we happen to be

living in the same house with a man who is murdered is no reason why
we all have to be treated like criminals."

"Now, Mr. Lingle," Polly interposed good-naturedly, "sit down and
relax."

"Relax! I feel as though I'll never be able to relax again. Not in this
house at any rate. Troy, you know about these things; could Hankins
keep any of us from leaving?"

Polly answered for Jeff. "If I were you I wouldn't give Hankins the
satisfaction of knowing he had any effect on me. That's just what he
wants—to unnerve us."

"There's something in that," Lingle admitted, cooling off a little.
"But if that policeman comes lumbering into my place once more,
I'm going to treat myself to some Mexican art—at the point of its
conception."

"If you're running away from the scene of the crime," Jeff said,
"Mexico is a bad place to run to. There've been enough precedents to
make crossing the border a suspicious move."

"Yes," Lingle said thoughtfully, "I see what you mean. I suppose I'll
have to stay here." He laughed self-consciously. "And, what's more,
I'll try to stop grumbling."

Polly sighed. "What we all could use right now is a change of address. A nice new change of address."

Jeff's exclamation made her stop. Mr. Lingle and I joined her in
staring at him. He had leaped to his feet and was standing in the middle
of the room as he drew an imaginary rectangle in the air with his right
forefinger.

"Change of address!" he shouted.

He got through the door with one jump and was pounding down the
stairs. I took one look at the astonished faces that gaped after him and
decided not to try and explain my husband's eccentricities. I followed
him.

But, only being able to take three steps at a time, I fell so far behind
that when I finally reached the sidewalk before number thirty-nine, Jeff
had already disappeared around the corner. And I didn't know which
corner. So I acknowledged defeat and went back home.

For the next hour I drew imaginary rectangles in the air and shouted,
"Change of address!" It didn't do any good. I could make nothing of it.
I would just have to sit and wait for Jeff to return.

The way he bounced into the living room told me that something had happened.

"Haila!"

"What?"

"Haila, Jacob Bruhl!" he gloated. "Now I know!"

"Know what?"

"His letters—where they go, why, how it works! It's so simple!"

"Where have you been?"

"To the post office. The post office from whence come the little men who collect letters which are mailed in the vicinity of this house. That letter I wrote, for instance. And 507 West Twelfth Street is served by this same post office."

"Jeff—uh—pardon me if I appear sane, but what are we getting at?"

"This. How does Bruhl get mail from Polly Franklin and George Turner addressed to 507 West Twelfth Street when he doesn't live there—has never lived there?"

"I know. He doesn't get it. All his letters are in the Dead Letter office."

"No, Bruhl gets his mail."

"But how? Nobody at West Twelfth Street forwards it to him. The letter never even got there."

"Right."

"Jeff," I said plaintively, "will you tell me? Please?"

"Listen. Mail is now being sent to our address in Connecticut. But it won't ever get there. The people who are living in our house now won't ever see it. It'll come straight here. How did we manage that?"

"Of course!" I yelped triumphantly. "Bruhl registered a change of address at his post office. His mail goes directly from the office to another address."

"Sure. Without ever having to go near 507 West Twelfth Street or having anything to do with it, Bruhl could give it to Turner and Polly as his address. Then he could go immediately to the post office and register a change of address. He gets his mail. And at a place that none of his correspondents know about, evidently."

"But why would he go to all that trouble?"

"I wonder, Haila, I wonder. Let's go and ask Mr. Bruhl himself."

"Where is he?"

"I had to make a nuisance of myself, lie, deceive, and impersonate to find out from the post office. Mr. Jacob Bruhl's actual address is 14 Tilton Court. Which is right handy, just below Bleecker Street."

In the hallway we were slowed to a standstill by Charley. But it was worth it. Charley was the bearer of great news. Our lock was to be installed within the hour.

"Charley," I said, "will you be here when the man comes? Will you see to it personally that the lock goes on *our* door? That lock—I don't trust it."

"I'll be cleaning the hall all afternoon," Charley promised.

"Haila!" Jeff was urging. "Come on!"

"Thanks, Charley. At last a lock!"

"There will be three keys," the little janitor called after us. "I got you an extra one!"

"An extra one! Charley, you're wonderful!"

"So are you, Mrs. Troy!" Charley yelled.

At the corner Jeff stopped to hail a cab and I managed to catch up with him. "Jeff, don't let's ride. Let's walk to Tilton Court."

"Why? Aren't you in a hurry to meet Bruhl?"

"Not too much," I confessed. "Frankly, this isn't joy I'm suddenly trembling with."

"Take my hand, Haila."

I did just that. But it didn't help much. Jeff wasn't shaking exactly, but I wouldn't have trusted him, at that moment, to cut the Hope diamond.

CHAPTER FOURTEEN

TILTON COURT WAS ONE of those short dead-end streets that hide themselves aloofly in the middle of New York's blocks. A row of tall, narrow houses lined each side of the so-called court, and tiny rectangular spots of lawn separated them from the sidewalk. Shrubbery and window boxes added to the pleasantness of the place and, undoubtedly, to the rent.

Number fourteen stood out from the other houses for it was a half-story taller than its neighbors. Beside the door there was only one bell. Jeff reached out and pressed it.

We waited a long time and there was no answer. Jeff raised his hand to ring again. But before his thumb touched the button, the door began to open. It stopped when it had crept back a scant three inches and a voice from behind it challenged, "What do you want?"

"Is Mr. Bruhl at home?" Jeff directed his question through the non-divulging crack.

"No," the voice said. Although it seemed to have no intention of saying more the door remained ajar.

"Are you expecting him?"

It was a second or two before the voice replied.

"Who are you?"

Jeff's hand reached out to grasp mine and pinch it warningly. "Turner," he said. "George Turner."

I had to repress my look of astonishment instantly for the door had opened now, and we were face to face with the owner of the voice. She was a tall, statuesque woman in a yellow velvet negligee, almost flamelike against the darkness of her background. Her hair was murky black, pompadoured elaborately in front and hanging to her shoulders in

126

back, her wide, slightly vacant eyes were black-fringed. She was what made the boys stop turning the pages in *Esquire*. And she was not what we had expected to find behind that door.

She looked at us searchingly. "George Turner," she repeated, as if she were striving to remember where she had heard that name before. Then, without moving her head, her eyes were on me. "And who is this?"

"An old friend of mine," Jeff answered. "Would you mind if we came in and waited for Mr. Bruhl?"

She shrugged. "It's up to you. I don't know when he'll be back."

"We'll take a chance," Jeff said.

We followed her through a short hall into the living room. There the light from several soft-shaded lamps fell on *moderne* furniture, that squat, square design that lures glamour-minded wives into the installment plan. Stunted chairs and a long, low davenport upholstered in a nubby oyster-white. Tricky cabinets and shelves and a revolving coffee table in bleached mahogany. Draperies and rugs of violent, blazing color. At the far end of the room was a curling white-banistered staircase and at the other a fireplace with an ornately carved mantel.

The woman nodded us into chairs while she draped herself on the arm of the davenport. I found myself comparing her to Polly Franklin, for they both had that same lusty, almost animal quality about them. But there was a warmth and a roundness in Polly, a kind of graciousness and dignity. This woman was of a minor key, brooding and dark, but a little too hard to be tragic. The impatience with life that showed in her heavy-lidded eyes had twisted her full mouth into petulance.

She sat waiting for Jeff to speak, and at last he pulled himself together enough to manage a few words.

"I hoped Mr. Bruhl would be at home."

"He isn't," she said curtly, still waiting.

"Are you Mrs. Bruhl?"

Her laugh was short and brittle. "No! This is my house and I rent Bruhl an apartment on the fourth floor. That," she added emphatically, "is the way it is. And not the way you're thinking."

"I'm not thinking," Jeff said. "I'm not thinking anything."

"It's a big house. Very big. Sometimes I don't see Bruhl for days."

"He isn't always here?" Jeff asked quickly.

"Some weeks he just drops in to pick up his mail."

Jeff almost leaped out of his chair. "You mean he just uses this place for a mailing address?"

She looked frowningly at him for a long time before she shrugged and said, "Maybe. I never thought about it. Maybe he does."

"Or maybe he just stays here long enough and often enough to keep you from thinking that?"

"Listen! If Jake Bruhl is mixed up in anything, I don't know about it!" She got up and strode over to the coffee table for a cigarette. But it wasn't a nervous gesture; there was nothing remotely resembling nerves about this baby. "I don't know a damn thing about Jake Bruhl's private life."

Jeff said, "That my name is George Turner seemed to mean something to you."

The woman smiled, a strange, slow smile. "I know your name, Mr. Turner. I've seen it on the letters you've written to Bruhl. Return address."

"Have you ever noticed the names on any other letters?"

"Well, now, let's see—a Polly Franklin, I think, writes to him often. And a person named Carstairs, Scott Carstairs. There's a Henry Lingle and a—someone named Griffith."

I smothered my gasp before it got too far. Not only Polly and George Turner were having dealings with this man. Scott and Henry Lingle and the Griffiths—all of them, everyone in 39 Gay Street was connected in some way with Mr. Jacob Bruhl.

"Does the name Michael Kaufman," Jeff was asking, "mean anything to you?"

"No." The reply came with great positiveness. "There was never a letter from anyone named Kaufman."

Jeff grinned at her. "You're pretty well acquainted with Mr. Bruhl's mail, aren't you?"

She exhaled smoke angrily. "All right, I might as well admit it. I'm damned curious about Bruhl myself. I can't figure out what his racket is. Maybe you can tell me. I've seen him take money—cash—out of those letters he gets. What's he selling, anyway?"

"Well, now—" Jeff faltered.

"Why don't you tell me? You know, Turner. You've sent money to him often enough. I've got a right to know. The man's living in my house! I don't want to get in any trouble."

"Listen," Jeff said. "You tell me some things I want to know and I'll tell you all that I can about Mr. Bruhl. You may be first. What does Mr. Bruhl look like?"

She calmly examined Jeff from under her lowered lids. Then she smiled. It was a sly, unpleasant smile. "He's definitely not my type," she said. "Stocky and short and dark. His hair grows almost down to his nose. And there's a droop in one eye that always gives me the willies."

Jeff throttled my exclamation. "Yes, Haila," he said. "Now we know. Jacob Bruhl."

Now we knew for sure what Jeff had suspected from the beginning. There was no Michael Kaufman. That name had been only an alias for this man Jacob Bruhl. But my elation at learning that was short-lived. For who was Jacob Bruhl?

He was a man whom we had overheard as he was making a date for his own destruction; a man whose identity had been skillfully obliterated by his murderer; a man who lived in an apartment at 39 Gay Street under the name of Michael Kaufman and who rented an apartment on Tilton Court to collect the money he was receiving from his Gay Street neighbors.

Jeff was intent on learning more. Moving closer to our hostess, he asked, "How long has Bruhl been living in your house?"

Her answer came promptly. "Four years."

"How did he happen to rent your apartment? Did you advertise it?"
"Yes."

"What paper? What date?"

The woman's head jerked up. The vacant, open look left her dark eyes, and a wariness crept into them. It was then that I saw that her hands were trembling and her whole body had become taut, excited. "No. No, I'm wrong about that," she said. "It's been so long ago that I forgot. I met Bruhl through a mutual friend. I didn't advertise."

"What's this mutual friend's name? I bet he could tell us about Bruhl. How did it happen that you never asked him? Since you've been so curious about your tenant?"

"I—I never got around to it."

"I see," Jeff said. He started walking rapidly toward the stairway, talking as he went. "You won't mind if I take a look at Bruhl's apartment, of course. There might be something—"

"No, you can't!" The woman screamed the words. "You can't, I won't let you!"

Jeff was already on the stairs, taking them three at a time. The woman raced across the room and up the steps after him, stumbling and floundering on her long negligee. Following, I could hear her choking gasps as she climbed. It was a ludicrous, fantastic chase that I couldn't believe was happening, that I couldn't make rhyme or reason out of. But I kept plodding up the stairway.

Jeff reached the top long before either the woman or I. He was standing in a room on the fourth floor, waiting for us when we arrived. The room, the only one on the floor, was filled with trunks and boxes and old pieces of broken furniture. It was obviously only an attic used for storage. Jacob Bruhl's apartment, then, had been a myth.

Leaning against the door at the head of the stairs, the woman faced Jeff, her dark eyes shooting sparks of frightened fury. Her labored breath came hissing out between gritted teeth.

"So there isn't any apartment," Jeff said. "Is there?"

"No," the woman said. "Jake Bruhl lives here. It's his house. So what of it?"

"So you know plenty about him, maybe everything. And now I want to know."

"I've told you everything—everything I know!"

"Uh-uh." Jeff's voice was threateningly grim. "For instance, you know that Jacob Bruhl will never be back. Because you know that Jacob Bruhl is dead. His body, stripped, was found in the garden of 39 Gay Street yesterday morning. He was identified as Michael Kaufman. But you knew it wasn't Kaufman, didn't you? You knew that the dead man was Bruhl."

"You're crazy!" Her voice was hoarse and wild.

"You know about that money, too. The money that Scott Carstairs and Polly Franklin and Turner and Lingle and the Griffiths kept sending to Bruhl in that weird, untraceable way was blackmail money and you know that, too. Jake Bruhl was blackmailing all his neighbors at 39 Gay Street and that's the reason he's dead, murdered, isn't it?"

The way the color drained from the woman's face leaving it a pasty-white, the terror that sprang into her eyes was answer enough.

"You're not George Turner," she muttered, "you're from the police."

She must have mesmerized us both with those wide, staring eyes, for we watched her back slowly through the doorway onto the steps. And then it was too late. The door slammed as Jeff lunged at it from across the room, the key clicked in the lock as his hand touched the knob.

The sound of running footsteps on the stairs was almost drowned out by Jeff's futile kicks at the bottom panels of the door. He reared back and threw his weight against it. Even after his fifth try, its thick oaken solidity was unruffled. He turned away and toured the room, stopping at each of the three windows.

The back two opened on a sheer drop to the garden below. From the side one we looked across an areaway to the next house. Not as tall as this one, its roof was on the same level as our window.

I knew what was in Jeff's mind even before his hands began sliding the window to the top. I grabbed him.

"Jeff, no! You mustn't, you can't make it!"

"We've got to get out of here!" His right foot was on the sill, his hands grasped the window frame. He took a deep breath.

"Jeff, you'll fall! You'll never—"

"Don't look," he said.

I didn't. I closed my eyes and waited an eternity. Even then I opened them too soon. I saw him land, his feet hitting the very edge of the roof top, his arms wildly flailing the air to regain his balance. Then he toppled headfirst upon the graveled surface of the roof. I watched him scramble up, run to the fire escape at the rear of house, and start down it.

He wasn't gone very long, not more than ten or twelve minutes at the most. But the time I spent alone in that attic room had the nightmarish quality of stretching itself out endlessly. It seemed hours before I heard Jeff's familiar footsteps pounding up the stairs. He unlocked the door and pushed it open.

"Haila, how are you?"

"Lonely! What took you so long?"

"I got all tangled up in back yards and a strange cellar three houses down the block. And I had to bust open a window to get back in here. C'mon, we've got to hurry!"

"Why? Where—"

"That dame!"

I chased after Jeff. The first room we looked into on the next floor told us everything we wanted to know. A butter-yellow negligee in a heap on the white carpet. The drawers of a cream-colored bureau standing open, most of their contents still inside or spilling out. A closet door ajar and a gap in the line of luggage on the floor behind it.

The woman must have been out of the house almost before Jeff had got off the fire escape. She had left practically everything behind her. I could imagine her tearing off the negligee, slipping into a coat, tossing a dress into a suitcase to be donned later at some hotel. There hadn't been time for her to do much else.

"Well," Jeff said, "I'm afraid that's the last of her. We three won't meet again."

"But, Jeff, she can be traced and found, can't she? All her clothes, all these things in the house—"

"Hankins can trace her if he wants to."

"If he wants to! Jeff, she's connected with this murder, isn't she?"

Jeff was frowning. "She was the victim's lady friend, but I think that's all. I'm sure she wasn't on the inside of the blackmail. She couldn't have known what any of those people were being blackmailed for. She didn't know enough about it to realize that I wasn't George Turner until I practically told her so."

"Well, anyway, let's get out of this place. I'm nervous."

"Sure, come on. I want to get home anyhow and have a little chat. With the murderer."

"But how can you? You don't even know who he is. Or do you?"

"No," Jeff admitted. "But it's merely a matter of acoustics."

He started out of the room, and I caught him by the arm.

"Shouldn't you," I asked, "notify the police—let Hankins know?"

"Not just yet. He'll raise too much hell because we didn't bring him along in the first place. But if I could get the case all nice and solved before he learns about this, he mightn't be so mean to me."

"Solve the case! Jeff, that might take you weeks—forever!"

"And, if I'm lucky, it might take a couple of hours. Haila, look. Now we know who the victim was. We know the motive for his murder. And more important than all of that, I've got the answer to his missing furniture. In fact, I've got everything but the name of the murderer. And I have a hunch that before very long—sometime tonight—we'll know that, too."

CHAPTER FIFTEEN

JEFF WAS NERVOUS. He threw his hat down on one of Polly's big chairs, pulled a pack of cigarettes out of his pocket, then decided not to smoke and tossed them into his hat.

"Polly," he said, "you could do Haila and me a big favor."

"Anything, darling. Anything at all."

"You could keep us from being eliminated, purged, done in. Simply by telling us which one of you murdered Mike Kaufman."

Polly's eyes and her mouth popped open. She stared at Jeff as if he were a ghost, a crazy, ranting ghost. "I?" she stuttered. "I—tell you— But I don't know! If I had any idea I would have—"

"Okay, Polly." Jeff picked up his hat. "We'll ask Charlotte Griffith."

"Charlotte Griffith? But she doesn't know, either!"

"And if she won't tell us," Jeff went on, "I'll ask Lingle or Turner or Scott Carstairs."

"Jeff, for God's sake, what are you talking about? They don't know any more than I do!"

"Polly," Jeff said, "you know. And they know. Every single one of you knows who murdered Mike Kaufman."

She stood looking at him, shaking her head in confusion. "No." She put her hands to her temples, pressing them hard. "Jeff, what are you talking about? What are you trying to say?"

"I'm saying that all of you have had a part in this crime. Maybe not in the actual committing of it, but in everything that went after. You know who Mike Kaufman was and why he was killed. You

133

know who killed him. And you're protecting the murderer. It has to be that way, Polly. It's the only way that Kaufman's furniture can be explained."

"Kaufman's furniture," she repeated dully.

"It never left this house; the police are sure of that. And yet they haven't been able to find it. You know the answer to that, Polly. They did find it, only they didn't recognize it. They thought it belonged in the apartments where they saw it."

"Jeff, that's stupid! It's—"

"Is it? Look, Polly, you have a big double bed in your living room and a small studio couch in your bedroom."

"I don't like to sleep on a double bed!"

"Not that double bed. Because that one belonged to Kaufman, didn't it? You divided his furniture among you. Each of you took the pieces that would fit unobtrusively into your own places. Scott Carstairs couldn't take much because Anne isn't in on this. He could only take a few books and—"

"Jeff," I said miserably, "not Scott! He hasn't anything to do with the murder, he couldn't."

"Scott's in with all the others," Jeff said grimly. "That explains his two copies of *Butterfield 8*. One of them was Mike Kaufman's, but Scott hadn't borrowed it from him. He had taken it after Kaufman was murdered."

"Jeff, no! There's some mistake."

Jeff didn't even look at me. "Miss Griffith," he went on, "didn't go out and buy the radio I saw in her room. She and her sister hate radios, they were forever complaining about the one Mike Kaufman had. It was his radio that I saw in their place last night. She didn't clutter up her Victorian apartment with those modern ashtrays and vases and bookends intentionally, either. Those things came from the dead man's room. Kaufman's stuff is all in your apartments, Polly, split up so that it's unrecognizable. A whole house could easily absorb two rooms of furniture and no outsider would know the difference."

Polly was looking straight into Jeff's eyes, mocking him. "You make it all sound so possible, darling. But so ridiculous. Why, in God's name, would all of us want to shield a murderer?"

"Because this murderer," Jeff said, "killed Jacob Bruhl."

The name had the same startling effect on Polly that it had always had. She sank slowly down on the bed, all assurance and bravura suddenly gone.

"The man who was killed," she said, faltering, "was Kaufman. Michael Kaufman, his name was."

Jeff shook his head. "No. That was only the name you knew him by. But later, after he was killed, you found out his real name. It was Jacob Bruhl."

She dropped her eyes quickly, but I saw the terror that had leaped into them. "Then you—you know about Bruhl?"

"Yes. I traced him to West Twelfth Street and from there to Tilton Court. I found out that he and Mike Kaufman were the same man and that he had been blackmailing all of you. One of you killed him and the rest agreed to protect the murderer. You—"

Polly stopped him. She drew one deep, steadying breath before she spoke. "All right, Jeff, you know. What are you going to do now? Tell the police?"

"I don't know. Death by drowning is probably too damn good for a blackmailer. I'm all for their extermination. But then I'm against people taking the law into their own hands, as the saying goes. And, just incidentally, of course, Hankins suspects me as much as any of you. More, maybe."

"But he won't—he can't ever do anything. He couldn't prove—"

"And there's another thing. Last night and the night before someone, your murderer, no doubt, broke into our place. Was he just seeing that Haila and I were tucked in our beds, Polly, or—"

"He wasn't trying to hurt you! I know about that, he told me himself! He knew that you were prying around, that you'd seen the name and address on the letter I wrote and that you were trying to trace Bruhl. We were all afraid that you might learn—what you have learned. We wanted to get you out of here. We tried to do it. Mr. Turner even offered to let you break your lease. But you wouldn't go. And so he tried to frighten you out. But that's all there is to it, Jeff, I swear that's all! You're not in any danger, I promise you!"

"I'd feel a lot safer though if I knew who the murderer was."

"I can't tell you!" Polly's voice rose, hysterical and shrill. "Can't you see that? Can't you understand that I'm helpless? The person who killed Bruhl has the same proof over us that Bruhl himself once had.

That's his hold on us. If we should make one move—if the police should find out anything at all—we'll all be exposed. We'll lose everything that we've fought so long and so hard to keep!"

"So the blackmailing has merely changed hands," Jeff said grimly. "Now you're getting it from Bruhl's murderer."

"But just for our silence, that's all. He has to do that, you can't blame him for that. Jeff, he isn't a criminal, not really! He—he *had* to kill!"

Jeff turned and walked to the window and stood looking out into Gay Street. For a long time there was no sound but the slow, thoughtful rhythm that he was beating against the glass with the knuckle of his index finger. Polly went to him and put her hand on his arm.

"Jeff, I can't take the responsibility of this on myself. Will you talk to the rest of them? Maybe there's some way—there's *got* to be some way—that we can get out of this."

"I hope so, Polly."

"I'll try to round them up."

Jeff stopped her at the door. "Anne Carstairs," he said. "She isn't in on it, is she?"

"No. She wasn't even here that night. And she didn't come home until it was all over. Scott kept everything from her; he thought it would be better that way."

Jeff nodded. "Anne knew that Haila and I were moving in here that night. If she had been one of you, the body wouldn't have been left in our garden. You wouldn't have put it there unless you thought the apartment was vacant."

"But Charley knew we had moved in," I said. "So he can't be involved, either."

"No," Polly said. "Anne Carstairs and Charley, they're both out. We would have kept Lucy Griffith out too if we had been able to. But we weren't. Jeff, you've got to believe me. If we had known that you, or anyone, was moving in that night, we wouldn't have used this place, we wouldn't have involved innocent people. But when we found out about you, it was too late. The—the body was in the garden and there was nothing we could do about it."

"We believe you, Polly. It was to your disadvantage to get us involved. And it would have been bad if Anne had found out what was going on. That's why you were watching her. You were afraid she'd find out. You watched her too closely and she felt it. She was frightened."

Polly said wearily, "Frightening Anne was just one of the mistakes we made. We were fools to think we could get away with it. But we were—we were desperate!"

"Yes," Jeff said.

"But if you—as far as the police are concerned, we're still getting away with it. Only you and Haila know. And if you—Jeff, please, will you talk to the others?"

"All right," Jeff said.

It was a long time before anyone appeared. There must have been a meeting of the mutual protection society in one of the apartments downstairs, for they all arrived together.

Polly, seeming to feel a responsibility as hostess of this macabre party, took up a position beside Jeff at the mantel. Henry Lingle sat nervously, tentatively, on the edge of a chair, the habitually smiling eyes clouded now with worry. Turner, his hands twitching uncontrollably at his sides, retreated as far into a corner as he could get, and Scott Carstairs sat on the arm of a chair, smoking a cigarette and eyeing Jeff with hostile distrust.

Miss Charlotte Griffith went directly to Jeff. "Mr. Troy," she said, "I hope you won't keep us here any longer than is absolutely necessary. Lucy is ill, much worse today. She couldn't be left alone, I—"

"I'm as anxious as you, Miss Griffith, that we get this over quickly."

"Thank you."

Miss Charlotte lumbered to a chair and, to my surprise, seated herself comfortably and began knitting away at a scarf. She might easily have been at a meeting of the Ladies' Aid Society.

A movement at the still-open door attracted my attention. Ward Franklin was standing there, awkward and puzzled. He swept the room with a baffled look and his eyes, finally landing on his sister, pleaded for an explanation.

Polly whispered to Jeff, and he strode across the room, pulling the door shut after him. In a minute or two, during which Ward's voice came angrily in upon us, Jeff returned.

"We've got to work fast," he said to Polly. "I don't think I've convinced your brother that he should stay away for very long."

"Yes, Mr. Troy, do let us hurry," Charlotte Griffith said, still busy with her knitting. I realized then that her absorption in her work was only to conceal her mounting nervousness.

"Anne's just around the corner," Scott snapped. "She'll be back any minute. What are you going to do about us?"

Before Jeff could answer, Henry Lingle was on his feet. "Wait! Wait just a minute, please. Mr. Troy, you know now who Mike Kaufman really was. You know why he was killed. But I want you to understand that—well, here is a houseful of people who were being persecuted, whose lives were being ruined by Jacob Bruhl. These people aren't criminals, Troy, they aren't murderers. Nor a menace to society. If you could—"

Turner's voice piped quaveringly out of the corner. "Can't you forget all this, Mr. Troy? Jacob Bruhl deserved to die; no one should be punished for his death. You don't punish people who kill rats! If you could only forget what you know!"

"Listen!" Scott said. He tiptoed to the door and flung it open. The hall outside was empty. Scott said lamely, "I thought—I was sure someone was out there." He sat down again on the arm of his chair.

Charlotte Griffith dropped her knitting and leaned forward. "I think," she said, "that if Mr. Troy were told what actually happened, he might realize—"

"Yes!" Polly's voice was eager, suddenly hopeful. "Yes, she's right. Jeff, listen to me. That man—he played with us like puppets, he drained us of every cent we could lay our hands on. He made us move into this house—"

Jeff interrupted her. "Made you move here? How?"

"A year ago," Scott said, "I got a letter from Jacob Bruhl. He said that the third floor at thirty-nine Gay Street was vacant. I was to rent that apartment immediately, before anyone else had a chance to. Unless I did that—Well, I did what he told me."

"My orders," Henry Lingle said, "came four years ago."

"Mine, three," Polly said bitterly.

Charlotte Griffith, her eyes staring straight in front of her, said, "My sister and I have lived here for two years. Lucy would be much better off in the country. It's bad for her here."

Jeff looked at Turner. "And you never knew that all these people had been sent to your house? That they were being forced to live here?"

"No! Oh, no! I never knew. I always thought they were just—just people looking for apartments. I didn't know that they had anything to do with Jacob Bruhl. It wasn't until after the murder that I—I realized anything."

"I see," Jeff said. "Living here in this house, Bruhl would know immediately when an apartment was to be vacated. But even then it took him three years to get you all in here."

"Mr. Troy," Charlotte Griffith said gently. "Mr. Troy, would you like to know why he made us live here? He even wanted to get his hands on the rent we paid and, through Mr. Turner, he could do that. And then, of course, disguised as Michael Kaufman, he was able to keep his eye on us. He could make sure that we were paying him every cent that we didn't need to exist upon."

"Sure," Scott said bitterly, "he could see that we weren't overeating or dressing too well or squandering money on vacations or books or theaters! That's why Bruhl made us live in this house. He was a coward, a nasty little—hiding behind a fake name, using a phony address, afraid to come out in the open."

"You can't blame him for that," Jeff said. "By remaining anonymous, he made the crime of extortion as safe as the mail-order business. You couldn't have reported him to the police or beat the hell out of him—even if you had dared to. You couldn't touch him in any way as long as he concealed his identity. But how did he work it that way?"

Miss Griffith hunched herself forward in her chair. "I'm going to tell you. Jacob Bruhl was a detective once. At one time or another he had a connection with each of us."

"But then you must have seen him."

"No, Mr. Troy. Bruhl was not hired by either Lucy or me; he was hired by Lucy's husband." She paused uncertainly and then, with a tightening of her lips, made her decision. "Mr. Troy, I am going to trust you. I am going to tell you about my sister and me—and Jacob Bruhl. Then you'll see that we, just like the others here, are not criminals."

The stout, motherly woman pushed her knitting needles into the ball of yarn and settled back in her chair. She was the only one in the room who was not casting furtive glances toward the door or suspicious ones at the other members of the group.

"My sister," Charlotte Griffith began, "married and went to live with her husband in—in South America. That's close enough. A few years later I visited her there. I found her in ill health. She hadn't been able to stand the climate and her condition was already dangerous. Her husband thought it was nonsense—I won't dwell on him, either—and refused to let her come back to the States. I had no money to take her back with me. Lucy had none. So I stole it from her husband, enough for passage and medical care, and I brought her back.

"He didn't get the police to bring us back. He was afraid of the scandal that would cause. But he hired a detective here to find us. And Jacob Bruhl found us. Then, instead of giving Lucy's husband his information, he began blackmailing us. We would pay him or we would be sent back. And so we paid him."

"That's what he did with each of us," Henry Lingle said. "Each of us has somewhere in our lives an equivalent to Lucy Griffith's husband."

Jeff nodded. "Yes, I see. A detective shadowing a person doesn't let himself be spotted. It was easy for Bruhl to remain anonymous to you. And, of course, out of the slew of cases he must have handled he handpicked you five. A smart guy, Bruhl. He had you all living under the same roof with him, and still managed to keep each of you thinking you were the only victim." Jeff shook his head in distasteful admiration. "But one of you finally traced him and tracked him down. You saw through his phony address and went to Tilton Court."

"Yes," Charlotte said. "One of us saw Mike Kaufman there on Tilton Court and knew that he must be Jacob Bruhl. Then one of us broke into Kaufman's apartment here and discovered that not only he, but everyone else in the house, was a victim of Bruhl's blackmail. That person robbed Bruhl of the proof of our various—mistakes.

"Then, somehow, Bruhl found out who had robbed him. He telephoned that person from Miss Franklin's restaurant and said to meet him in the basement apartment, thinking, of course, that it was unoccupied. He was going to kill him, you see. But he didn't disguise his voice well enough, and when that person came downstairs, he came prepared to meet a killer. So—" She stopped.

"So," Jeff said. "instead of Bruhl doing the killing, he was killed himself."

Miss Griffith said, "Yes. That's the way it happened."

Jeff looked around the room. "And the others in the house, how did they find out?"

Polly opened her mouth to speak, but Miss Griffith silenced her with a movement of her hand. "I'll go on. I'll finish our story. One of us coming into the hallway heard noises in your place and went to investigate. You know what he saw, Mr. Troy. A neighbor of his standing over the drowned body of Michael Kaufman. He screamed and the rest of the house came running."

"And then?"

"Then we heard the truth. Kaufman was Jacob Bruhl, our blackmailer. We—we were glad that he was dead and we agreed to help the person who killed him. At first we thought we would pretend that Kaufman had never lived here at all, that he was a stranger who had just wandered in somehow. But that wouldn't work because of Charley. He would have identified the body as Kaufman."

"I see now," Jeff said, "why you destroyed his identity. If the police were to discover that he was Jacob Bruhl they would also discover that he had been blackmailing you—and for what. And you wanted those secrets kept, of course. So you went to work to obliterate any proof that he—"

"Yes. His body was stripped and his clothes burned. We cleaned out his apartment and divided his things among us. Miss Franklin took the heavy pieces which would have been difficult to move down the stairs, his bed and his chairs. I took his radio and a lot of small things that might escape notice in my apartment. Mr. Carstairs could only take a few little things, books and the like, which he could hide from his wife. Mr. Turner took that atrocious screen and Mr. Lingle as much as his place could stand. Oh, we thought we were being very, very clever indeed."

Polly lifted her head defiantly. "We didn't do badly. Anne Carstairs never noticed anything and we had been afraid of her. We were always afraid that Anne or—or—" She stopped, fumbling.

"Or my sister," Charlotte Griffith said. "That's what Miss Franklin is trying to say. Lucy was ill to begin with. She hadn't the strength for an ordeal like this. She was frightened and wanted to tell the police. She tried to tell you on the stairway last night. Mr. Hankins had questioned her that day and she was near the breaking point. She had hysterics that evening. You heard her scream. But I've got her over the worst; I can manage her from now on. If you'll just give me the chance, Mr. Troy, if you don't go to the police with this story."

Scott Carstairs rose and stepped toward Jeff. "If you hadn't moved in here in the first place, things would be different. We would have been all right."

"We must have helped in a way," Jeff said. "At least we provided Hankins with two dandy suspects. We've kept his mind off the rest of you to a certain extent."

Scott laughed shortly. "You certainly didn't keep his mind off me last night. The next time Hankins calls on me I'm supposed to have a damn good explanation for why Kaufman's book was found in my house. Otherwise, he says, I'm going to find myself in trouble. Or in a cell."

"We tried to warn you," Jeff said.

"Thanks, but I wouldn't have needed any warning except for you two. If Haila hadn't overheard Kaufman on the telephone at Polly's restaurant, if she hadn't heard him use the words *go downstairs*, Hankins wouldn't have decided that this was an inside job. The street door is always open and there was no lock on your apartment. Anyone could have gone in there and murdered Kaufman. We had counted on the police thinking that. But you narrowed it down."

A frightened whimper from Turner swung us all around. He was standing beside a front window peering cautiously down into the street below. A black car had come to a stop beneath the arc light on Gay Street. Out of it climbed Detective Lieutenant Hankins and his assistant, Bolling. They stopped to confer before entering the house.

"We'd better scram," Scott said. "If those cops walk in on this meeting—"

Turner was already sliding furtively out of the room and his tenants crowded close behind. I could see their anger and their shame at having to behave like criminals, for having to hide at the sight of a policeman. Polly grasped Jeff's arm as we got to the doorway.

"Jeff, what are you going to do about us?"

"I don't know, Polly. I've got to think."

"But you'll talk to me again before—"

"Before I turn stool pigeon? Yes."

We hurried down the stairs in an attempt to get into our apartment before Hankins and Bolling saw us. They were still standing on the sidewalk, their heads together.

A new lock shone in our door and a white envelope with *Troy* scribbled in large writing across its face lay on the hall table. I snatched it up, tore a corner off it, shook out a key, and unlocked the door. Jeff followed me into the bedroom.

A second later the two detectives banged their way into the building. They started with Polly and worked down to us. And they were obviously still at a loss. Jeff and I had to answer the same old questions, listen to the same old accusations, stand for the same old innuendos that it was not inconceivable that we were a pair of murderers. When they left us they were at the snarling point.

Jeff was sitting on the edge of the bed, his chin in his cupped hands, staring morosely at the screen that had been Michael Kaufman's. He hadn't spoken for minutes and, from the looks of him, it was possible that he might not speak for hours or even days.

I took the initiative. "Jeff, you aren't going to tell Hankins what we learned upstairs?"

"I didn't, did I?"

"No, but what about from now on?"

"I don't know."

"Jeff, the people in this house deserve a break! That fiend, Bruhl! Making their lives a hell on earth, twisting them around his dirty little finger. Whoever killed that man deserves a Nobel prize."

I was being paid no heed, not a bit. Jeff was talking, not to me, but to himself. "That screen—it belonged to Mike Kaufman. It didn't belong to Turner. It belonged to Mike Kaufman—" Jeff wheeled on me so suddenly that his attention was more startling than flattering. "Haila!"

"What?"

"Was it Tuesday night that the first attempt to get in here was made?"

"Yes, Anne was sleeping in the other room and—"

"Was it Wednesday morning that we went to Twelfth Street to catch the mail delivery?"

"Yes."

"You came home alone, remember?" I nodded; he rushed on. "Hankins and Bolling were in our apartment—right?"

"Right. But what—"

"Did you go out at all that day?"

"No, not till that evening when you and Anne and I went to find Scott."

"But Hankins and Bolling had come back!" Jeff was getting more excited as he talked. "They were here when we left for the League! And when we came home—"

"They were still someplace around," I remembered. "Waiting for Scott."

"Yes!" Jeff almost shouted. "And this morning when we went up to see Polly and while we were at Tilton Court, they were in the house. Correct?"

"Correct," I said in bewilderment. "But what does it all add up to?"

"Every time we've been out of this apartment the police have been somewhere around—Wait, now wait." He pressed the heels of his hands against his forehead. "That means the murderer couldn't—"

"Jeff!" I said sharply. "There is no murderer! You can't call the person who killed Bruhl a murderer!"

"Haila—"

"Can't you curb the detective in you? Do you have to know *who* actually killed him? Don't you see that it's better if we don't know who the person is?"

"Better for whom, Haila?"

"Everybody!"

"Is it?"

"Jeff," I said slowly, "don't you—don't you believe what they told us? What Polly and Miss Griffith and—"

"No."

"You mean they were lying? All of them?"

"Not exactly. They believed what they were telling us; they thought it was the truth. At least, all of them except the murderer thought it was."

"Except the murderer?"

"Haila, it's sweet and touching of you to befriend Mike Kaufman's killer. I hope he appreciates it and remembers it—when you happen to get in his way."

I thought that over for a minute and then made up my mind. "Jeff, you're being silly and super-suspicious. I believe every word I heard tonight. Mike Kaufman's murderer is no more a criminal than I am. We're perfectly safe! The case is over. We're going to forget it and get back to normal. Beginning now with a good night's sleep so that you can be at the studio on time tomorrow and I can start looking for a job acting. Here, I'll give you a key; you might get home before I do."

I took the envelope of keys that Charley had left for us out of my pocket. Three keys, he had said. That would be one for Jeff, one for me, and a spare for visiting firemen. I emptied the envelope into my hand. I stood staring at the solitary key in it. I shook the envelope again; it was empty. In my pocket I found the key that I had used to unlock the door. But it made two, just two.

"Jeff!" I said.

"What?"

I held out my hand to show him. "Charley said there would be three keys—and look!"

"Let's see the envelope!"

I tossed it to him and he held it to the light.

"Haila, it's been steamed open and resealed."

"Yes, you can see it has."

"It was out there on the table in the hall for God knows how long. Anybody could have—"

"Yes. Jeff! Somebody has a key to our apartment!"

"Haila, the murderer being such a pal of yours—you sure you didn't give him one yourself?"

"The murderer? He wants to get in here?"

"Um-hum," Jeff said. "Why don't you bake a cake for him and—"

"Jeff, stop smirking! I admit I was wrong; maybe this case isn't over. Maybe the murderer is a—a murderer and—"

"Murderers are murderers. The world over."

"Well, what are you so happy about? Are you glad he's going to come creeping in here tonight and throttle us in our sleep? I've admitted you were right, haven't I? Now let's do something!"

"Haila, did you know that the Brevoort Hotel is one of the oldest hotels in New York City?"

"I knew it was no chicken." I made a beeline for the closet and dragged out an overnight bag. "And I'm staying at the Brevoort before it gets a day older. C'mon! Where are your pajamas?"

"Are you scared, Haila?"

"Yes, aren't you?"

"Just anxious. For your safety, darling."

"Me, too. I mean all my thoughts are of you, Jeff."

"Danger brings people closer together, Haila."

"I wish we were farther apart." I snatched the pajamas from Jeff's hand and threw them on top of what little I was packing in my haste to evacuate.

Jeff said, "I'll get our toothbrushes."

"Don't leave me here alone! Suppose the murderer comes in while you're in the bathroom?"

"Pretend you don't see him. And whistle Beethoven's *Ninth* three times so I'll know to stay in the bathroom."

Two minutes later, we were packed and ready to go. I snatched my purse off the dresser, jammed myself into my coat, and started for the door. Jeff slammed it shut behind us.

"Careful!" I whispered. "Do you want him to hear us?"

"C'mon," Jeff said. "Hurry!"

CHAPTER SIXTEEN

I HAD TO RUN TO KEEP UP WITH JEFF as he raced along Gay toward
Christopher Street. He shouted to a taxi a half block away. It charged
up to us, and Jeff shoved me into the back seat. He was following me in
when he said, "Damn!"

"What's the matter?"

"I'll have to go back; I forgot my wallet."

"I have money, Jeff."

"Sure?"

I opened my purse, rooted around in its depths, and succeeded in
digging up a measly ninety-three cents.

"I had a ten-dollar bill in here."

"You thought you had. But you've got enough for the cab, so you go
on. I'll follow you. Register in your right name so I'll know."

"Jeff, I can wait here for you!"

"No, Haila!"

He slammed shut the door, gave directions to the driver and tore
down Gay Street. The cab lurched toward Sixth Avenue. I settled back
in resignation. Then I was sitting bolt upright, banging at the glass in
front of me and shouting at the driver.

"Stop! Stop right here!"

Pouring my ninety-three cents into his hand, I jumped out of the
cab and then I, too, was tearing back toward number 39, my bag

clanking against my knee as I ran. That swindler, Jeff Troy!

While I was packing he had stolen that ten-dollar bill out of my purse—leaving me just enough change for cab fare to the hotel. He had lured me out of the house, tricked me into a taxi, and started me away so that he could sneak back and keep our date with the murderer alone. I was supposed to wait in the Brevoort Hotel while my only husband tried to make a widow out of me. I was supposed to wake in the morning to discover it was all over—one way or another. I was—But this was where I was getting off.

Once inside the narrow, crooked canyon of Gay Street, all the traffic noises from Sixth Avenue and up toward Sheridan Square were blotted out. It was deadly quiet. There was only one lighted window on the whole length of the short street, and that was high up under the roof of the old brownstone opposite our place. As I looked at it, it flicked out. Now there was no sign of life at all. Except for the arc light down the block, I might have been on a deserted street in a deserted city.

For just a second I hesitated in front of 39. Then I ducked down the steps, hurried through the hall, and knocked softly on the door of our apartment.

"Jeff!" I whispered with my lips close to the paneling. I didn't want a clout behind the ear. "Jeff, it's Haila!"

Without a sound the door opened, and I stepped into our bedroom. The door closed behind me.

Blankets had been draped over the two windows, shutting out all the light that usually filtered into the room. It was very dark. And it was so still that my breathing seemed to make a rumbling sound.

"Jeff," I pleaded, "say something."

"Why in hell did you come back?"

"Because I love you, Jeff, I had to. I love you."

"Oh, shut up. Darling. And go sit down and keep quiet."

"Where would be the best place for me to be?"

"Hah!"

"I know," I said quickly. "But I mean here. I want to help."

"All right. Go into the middle room."

"No, Jeff, I won't be any help out there."

"You'll be out of the way and that'll help. Haila, please go in there and sit in a corner. If anything should happen to you—Stay there and don't make a sound no matter what goes on out here. Go on."

He pushed me gently into the middle room, then tiptoed back to his ambush behind the bedroom door. I groped around until I found a chair, plunked myself into it, and took my bearings.

In back of me was the doorway into our living room. The lights from a stairway of a building that faced Sixth Avenue came through the French windows and made it possible to distinguish the outlines of the furniture there. But in front of me, and on each side, there was utter blackness.

"Haila!" Jeff said. It was a whisper that I could hardly hear.

"Yes, Jeff?"

"Okay?"

"Okay."

"We won't talk any more. The rest is silence, baby. I think I hear someone coming. Hold tight now."

I held tight. I held the sides of my chair and sat there motionless, listening, waiting. And then I heard what Jeff had heard. Footsteps coming down the stairs. They grew louder as they approached. Even-paced, unhurried. I clutched the chair and held my breath. They were on our floor now. Then I heard the outside door open and the sound of the footsteps fade away on the street. I let out my breath and relaxed.

I won't ever know how long I sat there after that, waiting for something to happen. I began to believe it had been the better part of my life. My legs grew cramped and my back ached. My eyes began to burn from the unblinking staring I was doing toward the blackness of the bedroom. I wanted a cigarette, I wanted to move around. I wanted to talk to Jeff.

Little sounds only accentuated the silence. Creakings in the house above me; a sudden rush of air down the fireplace in the living room, a war two cats were waging five or six fences away. But no more footsteps, no opening or closing doors, no sound at all from the bedroom where Jeff was waiting.

I wriggled around so that I could face the living room and look out into the garden. I could see the little concrete boy and his fish, both looking cold and forlorn. The only movement out there was the swaying of the slender sumac tree and the shadow of its branches on the windows.

If our murderer were the perfect criminal now, I thought to myself, *this is the way he would make his entrance tonight.* While Jeff waited, tense and ready, at the hall door in the front room, he would crawl through a garden window. Of course he wouldn't be able to risk the noise of breaking window glass and forcing locks. He would have had to arrange for the window to be already opened—

I felt an icy chill chase up and down my spine and the duck bumps pop out on my arms.

If he could have arranged for the window to be already opened!

And why couldn't he? The key to our apartment had been in his possession all evening. While we were chasing after a taxi, why couldn't he have come in, unlatched a window, and then sneaked back out again.

It suddenly became imperative that those windows be securely locked. Very quietly, I slipped off my chair and began to move across the room, feeling my way with my hands and taking short, shuffling steps. I kept my eyes fastened on the windows, watching for any movement outside them.

I was halfway across the living room when I saw it. At first I thought it was a moving shadow of the sumac tree. But after another step I could see that it was something real, something that rested on the lowest rung of the fire-escape ladder.

I stood glued in my tracks, watching it. It made no movement; I couldn't tell what it was. Without turning my eyes away, I stage-whispered to Jeff. There was no answer.

I tried again. "Jeff! Jeff, come here."

Still I heard no sound from the bedroom. I was about to take a chance and raise my voice to him, when I heard him coming up behind me. Of course, he couldn't have risked answering me. I twisted around, but I couldn't see him. The middle room was too dark. I turned back to the garden, found the fire escape again, and kept my eyes on it.

At last I felt Jeff at my elbow. I raised my hand and pointed to the thing outside the window and then, braver because my husband was within reaching-distance, I took one step forward.

I caught the disgusted snort that rose to my lips just in time. That thing on the fire escape had not been a man's foot. It was a piece of paper carton, wedged between the bottom two rungs of the ladder.

Turning toward Jeff, I stretched out my hand to him. I was about to whisper an explanation when I heard the sound. The soft, cautious sound of someone moving in the bedroom.

The murderer was there; I could hear his stealthy movements. Jeff and I stood where we were, hardly breathing. Waiting, listening.

I knew what had happened. In those few brief moments, when Jeff had left his post in the bedroom to answer my call, the murderer had come in. He was in there now, creeping around, probably toward the bed where he expected us to be.

Jeff would never forgive me. I had gummed the works. Instead of Jeff being behind the door when the intruder entered, he was here in the living room with me. Instead of the murderer being on the floor with Jeff on top of him, he was—But I was suddenly glad I had muffed the plans. They mightn't have worked. By now Jeff might have been on the floor with the murderer on top of him.

I moved my head closer to where I thought Jeff's ear would be. "Jeff," I whispered, as softly as I could.

"Shh."

We stood there for what seemed an eternity. There were no more sounds from the bedroom. I began to shiver, no longer able to control my tenseness and fright. I reached out with my other hand for Jeff's other arm to steady myself. And then Jeff spoke.

"Haila!"

I clamped my teeth down upon my lips to keep the scream from escaping. I held my legs rigid to prevent my knees from buckling under me. And I felt the hot flame of terror rush over me, enveloping and flooding me.

Jeff's voice had come from the bedroom.

It was Jeff in the bedroom. It was Jeff who was moving about out there now. And this dark form beside me—this arm that I was clutching—*this* was the murderer.

He had been there, huddled in the shadows of our living room all the time. He must have crept into our apartment while Jeff and I were out. Jeff must have surprised him there. And he had been waiting silently there, waiting for a chance to—

If I could get to Jeff—I *had* to get to Jeff. I took one quick sidewise step and it was that step that saved me. The blow glanced off the back of my head but it served, momentarily. Sparks danced in front of my eyes, my legs crumpled under me. I screamed as I went down.

It was a moment or two before anything that followed registered on my benumbed brain. A lusty yell from Jeff in the other room. A crashing at the French doors. A squeaking rusty rattle of the fire escape. Feet pounding toward me and Jeff bending down by my side.

"Haila!"

"I'm all right—up the fire escape!"

I managed to get to my knees and turn toward the windows. I saw only the bottom of Jeff's legs as he pulled himself up the ladder.

And then, before I even knew what I was doing, I found myself out in the hallway, racing up the stairs toward the roof. If I could block the staircase and the door onto it, the murderer would be between us.

I was panting and stumbling, terrified that he wouldn't come down, more terrified that he would. I tried not to think, not to plan. I hung onto the banister and climbed.

I pushed open the top door and stepped over the high sill onto the roof. At first I could distinguish nothing but the usual rooftop maze, crooked chimneys and bulging skylights and sprawling, uneven walls. There was no movement on the rooftop, nor any sound. The low moaning whistle of a departing liner on the Hudson, the noises from the traffic in the streets below, the million sounds a city makes, seemed deadened and far away.

"Haila." Jeff's voice came from directly behind me. He was standing on the other side of the opened door, his back flat against the wall. He reached out his hand and pulled me to him.

"Jeff," I whispered, "where is he?"

He raised his arm and pointed to the four-foot parapet at the front of the building. For a moment I could see nothing. Then I jerked back, huddling closer to Jeff.

The lights from a higher building behind us on Sixth Avenue caught the figure of a man who was crouched behind the chimney, and threw his shadow against the parapet. The shadow was all we could see. It hung there motionless, grotesquely enlarged and distorted.

"He doesn't know that we've spotted him," Jeff said. "He's trying to get back into the house without being seen."

"He might—have a gun."

"If he had, he would have used it long ago. No, we've got him, Haila. He hasn't got us."

"Jeff, who is he?"

Jeff shot me a grim look. "He's a fellow named Bruhl. Jacob Bruhl."

"Jacob Bruhl!" I gasped. "No, Bruhl is dead! Mike Kaufman was Bruhl."

"No. That's Bruhl over there behind the chimney. Haila, go back downstairs."

"Oh, no, Jeff, I won't."

"All right." Jeff took a step forward, raised his voice, and spoke in sharp, staccato notes. "Bruhl, listen to me! I know that Mike Kaufman was just another one of your blackmail victims and that you murdered him. He had traced you to Tilton Court, as I did; he'd phoned you from Polly's and made a date to kill you. But you got him first.

"Then you told the others that Kaufman was Bruhl and that you, too, were a victim of his blackmail. You said that you had tracked him down and stolen his blackmail proof. And they believed you and agreed to help you.

"You made them obliterate Kaufman's identity. They thought they were doing it so that it wouldn't be discovered that Kaufman was Bruhl. Actually, you were afraid it would be discovered that he *wasn't* Bruhl. Then they would have turned against you and you would have lost their protection."

The shadow on the parapet was rigid. No sound came from behind the chimney where the man cringed. Jeff went on, speaking faster now as if he were talking against time.

"Your neighbors believed you, Bruhl, they swallowed your story whole. I did, too, until I remembered something Charlotte Griffith inadvertently gave away. She said that screen we borrowed had come originally from Kaufman's place. It was on that screen, Bruhl, that we found your name and address—the phony address.

"Tell me this, Bruhl. Why, if Kaufman had been the blackmailer, would he have made a memorandum of his own name and address? And why, since he was the only one who knew that they would mean something to the others, would he have displayed it so carelessly? The answer is that he wouldn't have; he wasn't Jacob Bruhl.

"That was your one slip—not noticing the writing on the screen when you moved Kaufman's furniture that night. You didn't know about it until you saw it in our place. You had to get it off before one of the others saw it and started thinking. That's what you were doing in our bedroom last night and the night before. That's why you drugged our cocktails. That's why you stole our key and tried again tonight when you thought our apartment was going to be empty for the night. You needed time to obliterate that evidence, for the writing had been shellacked over."

Jeff had taken another step forward and was speaking louder and faster now, straight at the silent shadow on the wall.

"And your woman on Tilton Court, Bruhl. I know why she was so glib, so eager to give me all the information I wanted. Why she was so willing to talk about letters with money in them and return addresses. Why she gave me such a good description of Jacob Bruhl. She did it because she was playing a part—a part that you had carefully rehearsed her in. You had to do it, didn't you? You couldn't be sure that one of the people in this house might not suddenly doubt your story and go to Tilton Court to check upon you. You had to be prepared for that. And that was why the woman described Bruhl to me as Mike Kaufman. That was why she included your name in the list of letter writers. She believed me when I said I was George Turner. She thought I'd come to check up on my blackmailer and she played her part for me, only she played it a little too well.

"It all adds up, doesn't it, Bruhl? And when those people downstairs who have been lying and sweating to protect you are told that they've been doing it for Bruhl himself, they'll stop protecting you. They'll go to the police and—"

Before we could move, the shadow on the parapet jerked and danced. The man darted out from behind the chimney, heading wildly for the edge of the roof. Just as he flung himself into space his body twisted and I saw that Jacob Bruhl was Henry Lingle.

CHAPTER SEVENTEEN

IT WAS ALMOST NOON the next day when Anne came down. She was shaky still, and pale, but for the first time the fear was gone.

"It's going to be all right, isn't it, Haila?" she asked. "The police know that Lingle was the murderer. His suicide proved that. They won't care about the—the rest of it?"

I shook my head. "They don't know there is any more to it. The crime's been paid for and it's closed now, finished."

She leaned forward suddenly. "No, it's not quite finished. There's something I want you to know, that you deserve to know. I want to tell you why Scott's been paying blackmail."

"Anne, don't tell me. I don't care. I don't believe Scott could have done anything criminal and—"

"That's just why I have to tell you, Haila, Scott's completely innocent. It was for me he got involved in the murder. It was because of me he's been paying blackmail."

"Anne! You?"

"It happened before I met Scott. While you were on the road, Haila, with some play. There was a murder, you may remember it. It was very unoriginally called the penthouse killing."

I did remember it, vividly. Even the papers west of the Mississippi had been full of its details. "Yes," I said slowly. "A man murdered on a terrace, shot through the head. There was a girl involved and she had

155

disappeared—" I stopped, appalled, as I realized what Anne's story would be.

"Yes, I was the girl. I was there in his place, but when I left he was alive." She spoke breathlessly, as if she were trying to get to the end before her courage gave out. "I didn't know that he had been killed until I read about it in the papers—and I read that the police were looking for a girl—an unknown girl. Me. I knew I should go to them and prove to them that I had nothing to do with the murder. But I was afraid—afraid that I couldn't prove it. The evidence against me seemed so damning. And so I—I kept quiet, and after a while it all died down and was forgotten. They never found the murderer.

"Then, two years ago, after Scott and I were married, Scott got a letter from Jacob Bruhl. He'd been hired by the victim's family, the letter said, and had worked on the case. He'd found something that the police had overlooked. A note I'd written to that man saying that I would be there the night of the murder. Unless Scott paid him, Bruhl said, he'd take the note to the police."

She sat there quietly, her eyes on her hands that lay clenched in her lap. She took a deep breath to steady herself and forced her hands apart.

"That's all there is, Haila. Scott paid Bruhl. He didn't tell me until this morning. He knew I wouldn't have let him do it, I would have gone to the police and told them everything before I'd let him—Well, I didn't know. I sat up there and sulked and suspected him of—of everything but the right thing. And all the while Scott was—" Her voice grew ragged and it cracked. Her head went down into her hands and she was silent.

"Anne," I said, as soon as I could manage it, "you've got a helluva swell young man."

Her eyes were glistening with tears but the smile approached the one that Anne had had a long time ago. "Yes. Thanks for—for understanding, Haila. And thank Jeff for me, too. The two of you and the two of us—Well, Scott and I are going to start living again. And elegantly, need I add? So long, Haila; Scott's waiting for me outside."

I was still sitting there alone thinking about Anne and Scott, when Jeff burst into the living room. "Well?" I asked him.

"Lieutenant Detective Hankins kissed me on both cheeks. He wants to adopt me and give me the best of care. Send me to the best schools, grade school, high school—"

"You're feeling much better, aren't you, dear?"

"The world is a much better place to live in now that Henry Lingle-Jacob Bruhl is out of it."

"Jeff! Where are the documents or records or whatever you call them that he used to blackmail everyone with?"

Jeff grinned and pointed to a little pile of ashes on the hearth. "I found them in his apartment and burned them last night. It took all my willpower to do it. There's blackmailing blood in me, you know. When I was seven and became bored with arson—"

"I don't want to hear about you, darling. I want to hear about Bruhl."

Jeff sat down and began unlacing his shoes. "Where are my old clothes, Haila? I've got to get the soil in the garden ready for fall planting."

"Listen! I want to know—how did Lingle get things on all those people?"

"Well, with George Turner it was the murder that took place here when this apartment was a speak. Remember, it was his testimony that led to Ziggy Koehler's acquittal. Bruhl worked on the case and he discovered that the testimony was pure perjury. Turner had been terrified by Koehler's gang into giving him an alibi. But Bruhl didn't turn that information over to the police. He filed it and used it later to blackmail Turner.

"And in Polly's case it was her child, of course. Bruhl was the first detective her husband hired to spy on her. And Ward Franklin wasn't quite right about his sister. She made one mistake, a bad one, right after her divorce. She was much too intimate with a married man and that would have easily proved her an unfit mother. But here again Bruhl didn't report his findings to his client. He kept them to use on Polly."

"Well, evidently that was Polly's only mistake. For we know that there have been other detectives at other times who've watched her and found nothing.

"And the Carstairses—"

"I know," I said. "Anne told me."

"And you heard Miss Griffith's story last night. The Griffith sisters were easy pickings for Bruhl, but it was Kaufman, our Mike Kaufman, who was his plum.

"Bruhl had been hired by an insurance company to investigate a suicide. He discovered what the company already suspected—that the death was not suicide, but murder, and the murderer was Mike Kaufman. But, as in all the other cases, he withheld the proof of the murder to use against Kaufman himself."

"But, Jeff," I said, "why weren't the police able to trace Kaufman then? Since that name wasn't an alias, after all?"

"But it was. He'd changed his name to Kaufman in an attempt to get out of Bruhl's clutches. But Bruhl caught up with him and his phony name and went merrily along with his blackmail.

"I suppose when Kaufman discovered the identity of his blackmailer at last, he didn't hesitate for a second to try and kill him. He was a murderer already. It isn't supposed to be hard to kill a second time. He tried and he got killed himself." Jeff ground out his cigarette and started for the garden. "I'll work in these clothes, I guess."

"You will not! Come back here, that's your best suit."

There was a knock at our door. It was George Turner and he looked ten years younger with the worry wiped off his face.

"Mr. Troy," he said, "I called the storage house. The bar will be sent over in the morning."

"What bar?" I asked.

"Listen, honey," Jeff said. "Mr. Turner is going to give us the old speakeasy bar. We'll set it up in its original place."

"Oh, we will?"

"Sure, it's only a little one. And it'll be wonderful! We'll re-create a page out of history!"

"And, Mr. Troy, about those murals—"

"What murals?" I demanded.

"Imaginative stuff, Haila! Great! One of them, as I remember, is called *Delirium Tremens*. The other is just called *Sex*."

"You'll need me to help put them up," Turner said. He swung around to me, explaining, "They cover each of the side walls in the middle room."

"Jeff," I pleaded.

"Now, Haila, Mr. Turner's giving you a new tub. Surely you don't begrudge me something I can use. When we come in from working in the garden, you'll need a bath and I'll need a drink and a glance at a nice mural or two."

"Jeff," I said, "listen to me! You can't bring those murals and that bar into this house! I forbid it! I absolutely refuse—"

There was another knock on the door. "Mr. Troy?"

"Yes?" Jeff called.

"Bank Street Stables!"

I collapsed in a chair. It was wrong of me to be angry. I should be grateful, deeply grateful. Our life at last had returned to normalcy.

THE END

About the Rue Morgue Press

"Rue Morgue Press is the old-mystery lover's best friend, reprinting high quality books from the 1930s and '40s."
—*Ellery Queen's Mystery Magazine*

Since 1997, the Rue Morgue Press has reprinted scores of traditional mysteries, the kind of books that were the hallmark of the Golden Age of detective fiction. Authors reprinted or to be reprinted by the Rue Morgue include Dorothy Bowers, Joanna Cannan, Glyn Carr, Torrey Chanslor, Clyde B. Clason, Joan Coggin, Manning Coles, Lucy Cores, Frances Crane, Norbert Davis, Elizabeth Dean, Constance & Gwenyth Little, Marlys Millhiser, James Norman, Stuart Palmer, Craig Rice, Kelley Roos, Charlotte Murray Russell, Maureen Sarsfield, and Juanita Sheridan.

To suggest titles or to receive a catalog of Rue Morgue Press books write P.O. Box 4119, Boulder, CO 80306, telephone 800-699-6214, or check out our website, www.ruemorguepress.com, which lists complete descriptions of all of our titles, along with lengthy biographies of our writers.